Dear Reader,

Have you ever run across an old childhood diary or a note you wrote in high school or college? It's fun and sometimes revealing to see what you were thinking when you were younger, what things were important to you.

The seniors at Women's Covington College who took the Sexual Psyche class (dubbed by the students as "Sex for Beginners") were given an assignment to write down their innermost sexual fantasies in the form of a letter to themselves. Their letter was to be cataloged with a code for anonymity and remain sealed for ten years, then mailed to them.

When Gemma White's letter arrives, she's just been blindsided by a divorce and is trying to pick up the pieces. The naughty words she wrote long ago stir a dormant desire and conjure up the image of Chev Martinez, the hunky carpenter who bought the fixer-upper next door to refurbish and sell. Exploring her fantasies with Chev helps Gemma reclaim her independence...but she hadn't planned on falling for the sexy transient!

I hope you enjoy *Watch and Learn*, the first book in the SEX FOR BEGINNERS trilogy. Don't forget to tell your friends about the wonderful stories you find between the pages of Harlequin novels. Visit me at www.stephaniebond.com.

Much love and laughter,

Stephanie Bond

STEPHANIE BOND
BOND
Watch and Learn

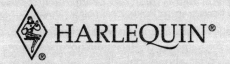

TORONTO • NEW YORK • LONDON
AMSTERDAM • PARIS • SYDNEY • HAMBURG
STOCKHOLM • ATHENS • TOKYO • MILAN • MADRID
PRAGUE • WARSAW • BUDAPEST • AUCKLAND

ISBN-13: 978-0-373-79432-4
ISBN-10:   0-373-79432-0

WATCH AND LEARN

www.eHarlequin.com

Printed in U.S.A.

ABOUT THE AUTHOR

Stephanie Bond's biggest heartache is that the beloved aunt who introduced her to Harlequin novels when she was a teenager passed away just before Stephanie's first Harlequin novel was released in 1997. Since that time, Stephanie has written more than forty romance and mystery novels, and doesn't plan on slowing down anytime soon, doing what she considers to be her "dream job." Stephanie lives in midtown Atlanta with her architect/artist husband.

This book is dedicated to all the people
at Harlequin behind the scenes, who work
so hard to bring so many great books to readers
all over the world.

1

GEMMA WHITE LOVED to make love in the morning. When the sheets were warm from lazy limbs, when muscles were rested and revived, when the day was yet a possibility. Morning lovemaking was an act reserved for the lucky few—new lovers who ignored the impulse to sneak out in the middle of the night, live-in lovers who still enjoyed waking up together, and married lovers wise enough to take advantage of a time when both partners' bodies were primed for passion.

Gemma smiled and rolled over, sliding a loving hand toward Jason's side of the bed. But when her fingers encountered cold emptiness, her eyes flew open and reality descended with a crash.

Jason was gone.

The desire that had pooled in her belly ebbed as sadness, temporarily banished by the cleansing arm of sleep, swamped her chest. The humiliation and shock of his departure hadn't lessoned over the past few weeks and, if anything, had become more embedded in her heart, like sets of bicycle tracks through fresh mud that had dried into an ugly, permanent cast.

Would mornings ever feel right again?

The wail of the phone pierced the air. She closed her eyes, cursing the person on the other end for intruding on her moment of misery. After four teeth-rattling rings, the phone fell silent…then started up again. Resigned, she swung her legs over the edge of the bed and reached for the handset.

"Hello?" she murmured into the mouthpiece.

"Are you up?" her best friend Sue demanded.

"Yes."

"Literally out of bed and walking around?"

Gemma pushed to her feet. "Absolutely."

"What's on the agenda today?"

"Um…" Gemma turned on a light and glanced around the cluttered bedroom. Dirty clothes occupied every surface. The floor was littered with at least two boxes of tissues crumpled into balls. "I thought I might…clean."

"Good. You want everything to look great in case you have company."

"Are you coming to Tampa?" Gemma asked, panicked. She wasn't ready to deal with the full frontal assault of Sue's personality. Her friend would roll into town from Tallahassee like a tank, armed with endless pep talks. But Gemma was too raw, too exposed, to deal with her failed marriage so matter-of-factly, over cups of frothy coffee and shoe shopping. She needed time to reorient herself.

"I can't get away from work right now," Sue said. "I meant in case Jason stops by."

Gemma tightened her grip on the phone. "Have you seen him? Is he coming here?"

"No, I haven't seen him. But in case he does drop by, you and the house need to look your best."

As if the divorce hadn't fazed Gemma. It was, after all, antifeminist to behave as if her husband's desertion had devastated her. Where was her pride?

"Have you told your parents yet?"

"No."

"What are you waiting for?"

"The divorce isn't final…yet."

"Gemma, you're stalling."

"It will break their hearts—Jason is like a son to them."

"Considering Jason's position in the governor's office, it's bound to hit the local papers soon. Is that how you want them to find out?"

"No." But neither did she want her mother pecking her to death with worry. "I'll tell them…soon."

"Did you find a job?"

Another dilemma. Unemployment was not so unusual for the wife of the state attorney general, but not so realistic for a divorcée with no alimony. "Not yet," Gemma admitted.

A noise outside drew her to the picture window overlooking the side yard. She nudged aside the filmy white curtain and looked down into the overgrown lawn of the empty house next door. A tall man with shiny dark hair was using a mallet to dislodge a faded For Sale sign that had been posted on the lawn for all of the two years that she and Jason had lived here.

"Have you even *looked* for a job?" Sue prodded.

"I will…today."

"Okay." Sue's disbelieving response vibrated over the line. "Gemma, you have to pull yourself together."

"I know, and I will. I just need some time to absorb my new reality." She pushed hair out of her eyes. From his tool belt, she gathered the stranger was a workman, hired, no doubt, by the new owner to fix up the place. She felt a spurt of relief for the sagging Spanish house whose exotic lines she'd always admired. But when the man lifted his dark gaze to her second-floor window, she dropped the curtain and stepped back, her face stinging.

The man had probably thought *her* house was empty. How many rubber-banded newspapers were piled on the front porch? Had weeds overtaken the brilliant birds-of-paradise and ginger flowers in the planting beds? Tending to the exotic plants that thrived in the lush Florida humidity had always been her favorite pastime. But since the final court appearance last week, she'd found it unnecessary to move beyond the front door.

"I'm sure any of the nonprofit agencies that you've helped to raise money for would be happy to hire you in some capacity."

"Probably. But I don't want to take advantage of my relationship with Jason."

"There's nothing wrong with using his name to get the job. You'll prove yourself once you get there."

Gemma understood the practicality of her friend's advice, but something inside her revolted at the idea of using Jason's connections. "I don't want to be in a position where I'd have to feel grateful to Jason, or be around people who might expect me to ask him for favors."

"I have some business contacts in Tampa. I could make some calls," Sue offered cheerfully.

Right—Sue's business associates would be *clamoring* to hire a thirty-two-year-old with an unused degree in art history. She'd save herself and her lobbyist friend the embarrassment of asking. "Thanks anyway. I'll find something on my own."

"Okay," Sue said warily. "Have a good day. I'll call you later."

Gemma returned the receiver with a sigh. She had no

right to be irritated with her friend. Sue was only trying to help in a situation that had rocked both of them to the core. Sue felt betrayed by Jason, too. She had introduced Gemma and Jason when the girls were seniors at Covington Women's College in Jacksonville and Jason was in law school at the University of Florida in nearby Gainesville. Sue had preened as her two friends had dated, fallen in love, graduated, married and evolved into an influential political couple.

I introduced them, she'd gushed to onlookers as camera bulbs flashed at their lavish wedding and over the years at every political appointment and election leading up to Jason being sworn in as state attorney general. When Gemma had called her, blubbering about a divorce, Sue hadn't believed her at first. Like Gemma, she couldn't conceive of Jason turning his back on their ten-year marriage with no warning and no remorse, as if it were simply one of the hundreds of decisions he had to make daily.

If there were fifty ways to leave your lover, he had surely chosen one of the most cruel. He'd asked Gemma to pack a suitcase for him for a last-minute trip and bring it by his office. Then after ensuring she had packed his favorite ties and shoes, he'd turned to her and said, "This isn't working for me anymore. I want a divorce."

Gemma remembered laughing at the comment. Jason had always exhibited a quirky sense of humor. But he'd leveled his pale blue eyes on her with an expression that she'd since realized was pity. "I'm moving to Tallahassee alone, Gemma. It's over."

It's over. As if he was referring to a television show or a song that had run its course.

A banging sound next door jarred her from her circular

thoughts. Gemma wiped at the perspiration on her neck, realizing suddenly that she was sticky all over, that the air in the room was stifling. A check of the thermostat revealed that yet something else had gone wrong when she wasn't looking. She'd have to call a repair service.

She went from room to room on the top floor to open windows, releasing heat that had risen in the house. The bedroom that Jason had turned into his office looked as if it had been violated, stripped of furniture and decorated with cobwebs in strange places. From the walls sprang naked cables that had once provided power to fuel his busy life.

It was exactly the way she felt. Unplugged and unwanted.

When she returned to her bedroom to slide open the side window, she chanced a glance at the house next door, startled when the peeling shutters on the round window twenty feet across from hers were thrown open and the dark-haired man she'd seen earlier appeared. She distantly registered the fact that she was wearing only a thin tank top and no bra, but she was rooted to the hardwood floor when his gaze landed on her. He inclined his head in a polite nod.

Gemma managed a shaky smile, but he was already gone, like the breeze.

Feeling sideswiped, her smile dissolved into an embarrassed little frown. A glance up at the sky had her shielding her eyes in mild surprise. In contradiction to the gloom hovering over her inside, it was a beautiful early spring day outside. The sun was everywhere.

She'd thought she'd be living in Tallahassee by now, settling into a new home close to Jason's new office, socializing in the governor's circle and generally being the helpmate that she'd learned to be…looking good, speaking well.

Being ignored.

The thought slid into her mind unbidden, and instantly she resisted it. She had been an integral part of Jason's life, had helped him achieve his dreams—*their* dreams. She had been relevant. Perhaps Jason had fallen out of love with her, but he hadn't ignored her.

Otherwise, how could she have been happy?

Frowning, Gemma turned away from the window and padded downstairs in search of something cool to drink. The kitchen was dark and hummed with electric white noise as the refrigerator labored to stay cool. The pungent smell of overripe fruit hung in the air. From a wire basket, Gemma picked a pear to munch on, then rummaged in the fridge, past Jason's Red Bulls, for a bottle of tea.

While she drank and waited for the caffeine to kick in, Gemma mentally sifted through the things that had unraveled, things she needed to tend to. Sue was right about one thing—she had to find a job. She was more fortunate than most divorcées in the sense that in lieu of alimony Jason had paid off the house and her car, and left her with a small savings account. But she didn't want to squander what money she had, and the house and car wouldn't run on their own.

Besides, a job would help her to…rebuild. Reclaim. Renew. Her future could be waiting for her in the Help Wanted ads.

She pulled on shorts and a T-shirt, and swept her hair back into a ponytail. Then she unlocked the front door and walked barefoot out onto the covered porch. The light gray painted wood planks were gritty beneath the soles of her feet, the two chairs sitting next to a small table full of leaves and yard debris. Scooping up the rolled newspapers, she turned and tossed them inside. Then she surveyed the weedy, neglected yard that would have to wait until she addressed other items on her mounting to-do list.

How quickly things could go from neat and orderly to utterly out of control.

She walked to the mailbox and, at the curb, turned to take in the house next door. The faded yellow, two-story stucco structure with the red tiled roof and wrought-iron details was one of the last houses in the older, eclectic neighborhood to be rescued. She thought she remembered hearing that the house had been tied up in court, something to do with probate. If properly restored, it would be glorious, she decided, much more interesting than the sturdy but standard home that she and Jason had settled into.

The dark-haired handyman was nowhere to be seen, but his presence was evident. The For Sale sign was gone and two ladders leaned against the front of the house. A pressure washer and other equipment sat near the front door. She smiled, relieved that the house would finally receive the attention it deserved.

Her mailbox, labeled "Jason and Gemma White, 131 Petal Lagoon"—another artifact of the marriage to correct— was stuffed full of high-tech catalogues and news magazines that Jason liked to read. It was taking a while for his forwarding address to trickle down. She loaded her arm with the mail and flipped through it idly as she made her way back to the porch steps. Her hand stopped on a large brown envelope with the county's return address. Walking inside, she closed the door behind her and dropped the rest of the mail on the kitchen table. With a sense of foreboding, she slid nervous fingers under the flap and pulled out a sheath of papers.

Final Judgment and Decree. Gemma swallowed hard

and scanned the four short paragraphs that officially terminated her marriage.

"...it is decreed by the Court that the marriage contract heretofore entered into between the parties to this case, from and after this date, be and is set aside and dissolved as fully and effectually as if no such contract had ever been made or entered into..."

As if the marriage had never existed.

Her eyes watered, blurring the words. This was it then. Proof that the last ten years of her life hadn't mattered. She'd assumed that she and Jason were years away from the menace of a midlife crisis, yet in less time than it had taken to plan her wedding, her marriage had disintegrated.

What now? she wondered, leaning into the granite counter, uncaring that the hard edge bit into her pelvic bone. TV therapists and girlfriend shows referred to breakups as a clean slate, a new chapter, a chance for a woman to find her authentic self.

But what if her authentic self was being Jason White's wife?

It was a notion that she didn't dare say aloud for fear that Oprah herself would appear on her doorstep. She knew that being absorbed into a man's life was considered passé, but she couldn't remember the person she'd been before Jason. She didn't have a point of reference, a place of origin. She recalled only a vague sense of floating aimlessly before she'd moored herself to him.

He had been her first and only lover. He was all that she knew.

The sound of the doorbell pealed through the air, jangling her nerves. She frowned, wondering who could be visiting. Then, remembering what Sue had said about having company, her pulse picked up at the thought that it could be Jason. Had Sue been trying to forewarn her? Perhaps he'd received his copy of the final papers, too, and he'd reconsidered...

Gemma wiped at the wetness on her cheeks as she hurried through the foyer and was smiling when she opened the door.

But at the sight of the man standing on the threshold, her smile faltered.

2

THE SHOULDERS OF THE dark-haired handyman spanned the doorway. His hawkish features and long, work-muscled arms were coated with a layer of gray dust. A tiny gold loop hugged his earlobe, and a black tattoo extended below his right T-shirt sleeve. She put him in his late thirties, and was both taller and bulkier than he'd appeared from a distance. Chiding herself for not checking the peephole before opening the door, Gemma took a half step back. The man's appearance made her suddenly realize how vulnerable she was here alone.

She had to start thinking like a single woman again.

"May I help you?" she asked, trying to sound firm.

"Sorry for the intrusion, Ms. Jacobs," he said, his voice low and as smooth as her worn wood floors. Still, her throat contracted in alarm.

"How do you know my name?" Her maiden name…her old name…her *new* name as mandated by a formal order in the divorce papers.

"It's on your mail," he said, extending a white envelope. "I found this blowing around in my yard."

She took the long envelope, feeling contrite. "Oh…I must have dropped it. Thank you."

"You're welcome."

He nodded curtly and made a movement to go, but after her abrupt greeting, she felt compelled to reach out to him. "Did you say *your* yard?"

"I'll be living in the house for about a month, until it's ready for resale."

So he was planning to turn a quick profit, then be on his way. "It's a beautiful place," she offered.

He nodded. "I've had my eye on her for a while, but it took some time to close the deal."

Speaking of eyes, he had nice ones. The color of raw umber thinned with the tiniest amount of golden linseed oil. She hadn't thought of her paints in years. "I've always admired the bones of the house. I'm glad someone thinks it's worth renovating."

"Chev Martinez." This time he extended his bronzed hand.

After a few seconds' hesitation, she put her hand in his. "Gemma Jacobs." Her old name—her *new* name—rolled off her tongue with astonishing ease. Conversely, the physical contact set off distress signals in her brain. His hand was large and callused, but his grip was gentle…the hand of a man who was accustomed to coaxing a response from whatever he touched. Awareness shot up her arm, and she realized with a jolt that he was looking at her with blatant male interest. She withdrew her hand, suddenly conscious of her appearance, sans makeup and wedding ring. She wasn't sure which made her feel more naked.

"Do you live here alone?"

She knew what he was asking—if she was single… available. According to the papers she'd just received, she was indeed single, but was she available?

The sounds of summer imploded on them. The buzz of

the honeybees drawing on the neglected ginger plants, the caw of birds perched in the fan palm trees overhead. "Yes, I live here alone," she said finally.

Another nod. "If the construction noise disturbs you, let me know."

"I will."

"Guess I'd better get back to work." He half turned and descended her porch steps.

"So...you're in real estate?"

His smile was unexpected, white teeth against brown skin. "No. I'm a carpenter, but I sometimes flip houses. How about you?"

An expert wife. "Unemployed art historian, which is why I fell in love with your house."

"Maybe you'd like a tour sometime." He was backing away, but still looking at her—all of her.

"Maybe," she said, hedging. Now that he was out of arm's reach, she was regaining her composure. There was something dangerously magnetic about the man. In a matter of minutes, he'd demonstrated an uncanny knack for extracting the truth from her.

He lifted his hand in a wave and walked away, his long legs eating up the ground. From the safety of her shade-darkened porch, Gemma watched him cross her yard to his, drawn to the way he moved with athletic purpose. His broad back fell away to lean hips encased in dusty jeans with a missing back pocket. He stopped next to a silver pickup truck parked in the broken-tile driveway and from the bed lifted a table saw, stirring the muscles beneath his sweat-stained T-shirt. He carried the unwieldy tool to the front door of his house and disappeared inside.

Gemma wet her lips, conscious of a foreign stir in her midsection—arousal?

Then she scoffed. That was impossible.

Stepping back inside, she closed the door and turned the dead bolt lock for good measure. Her reaction was mere curiosity…and pleasure that the house next door seemed to have acquired a good caretaker for the time being.

She liked the way he'd referred to the house in the feminine sense, as if he were restoring honor to a once-grand lady. The affection in his voice for something that he'd been willing to wait for left Gemma warm and wondering. Between his benevolence and his…bigness, the man was an intriguing addition to the local scenery.

Not that she knew many of her neighbors. Even though she and Jason had lived in the neighborhood for two years, their social circle had remained with Jason's law cronies and state government associates. Gemma had made a few acquaintances while working in her flower beds, but nothing past small talk and vague promises to get together sometime for a cookout. She'd known that if Jason won his bid for attorney general, they would be relocating anyway.

Now it looked as if she'd be living alone at 131 Petal Lagoon for the foreseeable future.

She sighed and glanced at the envelope her neighbor had handed her. Her maiden name and the street address were typed neatly in the dark font of a laser printer. The return address was a post office box in Jacksonville—no doubt a mailing from Covington Women's College.

Gemma gave a wry smile and tossed the envelope onto the table with the rest of the mail. She'd have to defer her annual donation to her alma mater until after she found a job and paid down her bills. With that goal in mind, she retrieved the bundled newspapers. While the logistics of finding a job seemed overwhelming at the moment, the idea of having her own career sent a flutter of nervous anticipation through her chest. How long had it been since she'd given her own ambitions more than a passing thought?

Since before Jason…since college.

Squinting, she tried to remember her goals before she had allowed herself to be absorbed into Jason's life plans. They must have been flimsy, she acknowledged ruefully, if she had been so willing to cast them aside. There had been many trips to art museums, she recalled, to make notes on traveling exhibits that she might never get to see again. Where were her journals? And she'd volunteered her services to catalog tedious bits of obscure collections that might or might not prove valuable someday, such as hand-drawn elevator door designs from the late 1800s and the tools used by mason workers to cobble the streets of Saint Augustine. Being around old things comforted her—the permanence, or at least the history, of objects made her feel as if everything in the world had some significance, herself included.

But the last time she'd been to an art museum had been for a political fund-raiser, where bleached smiles and glad-handing had overridden the more meaningful backdrop.

She opened a week-old newspaper and, after glancing over the headlines that she'd missed, turned to the Help Wanted ads.

"Art, art, art," she murmured, skimming the columns with her finger, thinking that a curatorial position would be nice, or something in art preservation. Or maybe teaching. Her finger stopped on an ad for an executive assistant for the director of a local museum. She smiled—maybe this wouldn't be so hard after all. The job description sounded interesting and challenging. Then she skimmed the requirements and pushed her tongue into her cheek. A master's degree, two to four years experience, and proficiency in computer programs she'd never heard of.

Still, it was worth a phone call. She dialed the number listed and after a series of automated selections was finally connected to a live person in human resources who informed Gemma that the job had been filled through an employment agency the same day it had been listed.

After browsing the ads of other, less appealing jobs available in the "arts" field and realizing that she was woefully underqualified for all of them, Gemma pushed to her feet. Crossing the kitchen, she fought a panicky feeling that was becoming all too familiar lately—the feeling that the exit she'd chosen in life had no reentry back onto the freeway.

In a word, she felt...*stupid*. And angry with herself. Thirty-two years old and she was suddenly ill equipped to live her own life.

Hoping that a pot of java would improve her outlook, she filled the coffeemaker and listened to it gurgle as she stared out the window at the house next door. With its shutters, doors and windows thrown open, the house looked vulnerable. Indeed, it seemed to be sagging in self-consciousness, as if the old girl were resigned to the idea that before she could be restored, she first had to be stripped of her pride.

And from the dust clouds buffeting out of the second-story windows, Chev Martinez appeared to be the man for the job. She craned for a glimpse of him, but the rude beep of the coffeemaker interrupted her idle musings.

Which was just as well.

CHEV MARTINEZ PAUSED and leaned on a push broom to allow the dust in the room—and in his head—to settle. He'd been anticipating this day for months, since he'd first spotted the Spanish-style house sitting abandoned, a fading exotic bloom in an otherwise bland but upscale neighborhood. Since that time, he'd driven by countless times, just to reassure himself that the place was still standing, still waiting for him.

And he'd become accustomed to seeing the fresh-faced blonde next door tending to her flower beds. He'd seen the husband's name on the mailbox, knew the man's title and position, and had tried to put her out of his mind. But there was something about the woman that spoke to him—the grace of her lithe body, the big hats and colorful gloves she wore gardening, the fact that she always looked as if she were humming.

She was…*happy.* Chev had envied the man who came home to her sunny smile every day, had imagined that she possessed a wicked sense of humor and was a great lover. The kind of woman who presented a proper appearance for the political scene and her suburban neighbors, but came undone in the privacy of her own bedroom.

When he'd pulled up today, he'd known something had changed. Her yard was untended and newspapers were piled on the porch. Her house was dark and quiet. His first thought was that she and her husband had taken an extended vacation, but then he'd seen a light go on in an upstairs room, had seen her solitary figure moving around. Knowing she was there had left him feeling antsy all morning. Finding the stray letter in his yard had given him a legitimate reason to knock on her door, but he'd paced around like a kid before working up his nerve.

With good reason.

Seeing her up close had sent his vital signs galloping. Her red-rimmed eyes and damp cheeks had confirmed his suspicion that something was wrong, and the tan line on her ring finger had given him a clue as to what. Her response that she lived alone cinched his suspicion that the woman's happiness had been brought to a halt by a sudden end to her marriage.

The knowledge both saddened and unnerved him. He'd met plenty of women for whom he'd felt a physical attraction, but there was something so...*appealing* about this woman that it disarmed him. He could see in her eyes how broken, how vulnerable she was, and while his first instinct was to get close to her, he didn't want to get involved with a woman who lived only a few steps away from his work site...and who was still holding a torch for her ex. Besides, he was only responding to the wild fantasies he'd spun about the woman. She was probably nothing like he'd imagined.

Gemma.

Of course her name would be unique, special. Of course she would recognize the neglected charm of this house. Of course her legs would be long and her breasts full. Of course she would have a brown beauty mark next to her shapely mouth that completely stole his concentration.

He pulled a handkerchief from his pocket and mopped at the sweaty grit on his neck. He had to get his libido under control and his mind back on the job. It wasn't as if Gemma Jacobs was looking to start up something with him. Her husband's policies hadn't been particularly friendly to Americans of Puerto Rican descent—for all he knew, she might share her ex's views. It was, he acknowledged, a flimsy attempt to distance himself from the woman in his mind, but he had a full plate at the moment and he couldn't afford the distraction.

This would be the third house he'd flipped in the past year. For someone who didn't own a house of his own—and didn't plan to ever settle down—he seemed to have a knack for knowing what home buyers looked for. He had one month to finish this renovation before he had to be in Miami for a lucrative commercial job. His goal was to put the For Sale sign back in the yard within that time frame and have a fat check in his hand before he left town. The auction was already scheduled. If he missed the deadline, he was screwed. Which meant there was no time to waste on a flirtation, no matter how tempting.

No. Matter. How. Tempting.

Forcing aside the thought of his neighbor's lush body, Chev walked to the window and ran a hand over the carved woodwork of the frame, some of it flaking paint, some of it rotted. This one repair alone would take hours, but in the end, it would be worth the hard work. People buying in this neighborhood would expect attention to detail. The place reminded him of pictures of his grandparents' colorful home in Puerto Rico. He took in the wide plank floors of the large room, the cracked plaster walls and ceiling, the tall rounded door openings, all of the finishes compromised from neglect and exposure to extreme temperatures. But the house would be grand once she was restored to her former self.

He stared across at the picture window where he'd seen his new neighbor this morning. Considering she'd been scantily clad and her hair tousled, it seemed likely that it was her bedroom window. A filmy white curtain moved with a light breeze, as if in confirmation.

Her window was larger and slightly lower than the one where he stood. At the thought of having a clear view of her bedroom, his sex hardened and pushed against his fly. Did she have flowery sheets? Did she like to sleep late? Did she ever sleep in the nude?

Chev turned away and shook his head to dislodge the image from his mind. He went back to sweeping, putting more muscle in it than necessary. He was losing his mind, playing with fire by indulging these dangerous fantasies. He made his living on the road, moving wherever the best jobs took him, satisfying his sexual urges with the occasional pretty barfly or waitress, partners who were as transient as he was. Not suburban divorcées who tended flower beds.

Besides, if Gemma Jacobs knew what he was thinking, she'd probably have him arrested.

3

AFTER POURING HERSELF a tall mug of coffee and adding milk, Gemma returned to the Help Wanted ads armed with a red pen. Several frustrating phone calls later, she had learned two things: jobs in the immediate Tampa area generally didn't remain open for more than forty-eight hours, and the majority of positions were filled through employment agencies. So when she spotted an ad for one such agency, she made another phone call.

A chipper sounding woman answered the phone and invited Gemma to come in the next morning for an "assessment of her skill set." Gemma made an appointment and hung up slowly, feeling as if she were back at the placement office on campus looking for work-study programs that would mete out enough to pay for toaster-oven meals and discount dresses.

When angry tears threatened to undo the progress she'd made, she turned her attention to the cleaning she'd told Sue she'd get to today. The house was musty and dusty and the laundry could no longer be ignored. Gathering cleaning supplies, she threw herself into the task, only to be derailed every time her feather duster encountered a photo of her and Jason, or when the vacuum cleaner unearthed relics of their relationship—a valentine that had fallen behind a table, a cuff link. The yawning emptiness of the house made it feel like someone had died. She considered making paper carnations out of the crumpled tissues littering the floor, but she had to admit, it felt good stuffing the tear-stained clumps into a trash bag.

The stack of things that Jason had inadvertently left behind continued to grow—a pair of golf shoes here, a wife there. Gemma made slow but steady progress, although she was hanging on to her emotions by a thread when the phone rang late in the afternoon. Seeing her mother's number on the caller ID screen did nothing to improve the day's direction.

But considering that her final divorce papers were on the table next to her *Real Simple* magazine, it seemed the moment to come clean with Phyllipa Jacobs was at hand.

"Hi, Mom."

"Gemma," came the wounded reply. "Is there something you want to tell me and your father?"

Gemma bit down on the inside of her cheek. "I guess you heard."

"You mean about my own daughter's *divorce?* A complete stranger at the local paper called to get my comment. I've never been so mortified in my entire life."

If the newspaper in the tiny town of Peterman had heard about the state attorney general's divorce, then it had to be on the wire services. Had Jason's office released a statement? "I didn't know how to tell you. I'm sorry you found out from someone else."

"Then it's true?"

"Yes."

"I don't believe I'm hearing this. What happened?"

Gemma dropped into a chair and gave a choked little laugh. "I really don't know."

"You're laughing?"

She closed her eyes. "No, I'm not laughing, Mother. I'm telling the truth. It was Jason's…idea. He wanted the divorce."

"*Jason* wanted the divorce? What did you do?"

Gemma flinched. "Why would you think I did something?"

"Because Jason loved you. He gave you a wonderful life."

"Mom, I—"

"Did you even *try* to work things out?"

The unexpected attack took her breath away. "Mom, Jason didn't want to work things out."

"That doesn't sound like the Jason I know."

Meaning Gemma didn't know her own husband—a direct hit. And true. He had fooled them all. Jason's parents were deceased, and her parents had welcomed him into the family like the son they never had. They had been delighted and proud that their daughter was married to such a powerful man.

"I know that you and Dad are disappointed, and I'm sorry."

"But what are you going to *do,* Gemma? How will you make it?"

She blinked at the utter certainty in her mother's voice that she couldn't survive on her own. "I'm going to get a job."

"Doing what?"

"I do have a college degree."

"That you've never used."

Gemma put her hand to her temple. "I'm sure I'll find something."

A baritone voice sounded in the background, then her mother said, "Your father wants to know if you need money."

"Tell him no, but thanks."

"Gemma," her mother said, lowering her voice, "if things were unsatisfactory in the bedroom between you and Jason—"

"Mom, don't—"

"I'm just saying that if he looked elsewhere for companionship, it doesn't necessarily mean that things are over."

"What's over is this conversation, Mother. I have to go. I'll call you soon."

She disconnected the call and dropped the handset as if it were on fire, still trying to process the surreal conversation. Her mother—the woman who had draped a kitchen tea towel over Gemma's face while she explained the birds and bees so she wouldn't have to make eye contact—was giving her advice on how to deal with a sexually unfulfilled husband?

Would everyone automatically assume that she was lousy in bed?

Probably, since she had jumped to the same conclusion herself.

Even in the beginning she and Jason had never lit up the sheets, but their lackluster sex life hadn't been an issue between them because they were compatible in so many other ways. They made time for each other…usually. His schedule had grown more demanding as the election had drawn near. But he'd sworn to her that no one else was involved in their breakup, and she wanted to believe him.

Two frantic days of tearing apart his desk, closet and credit card statements hadn't yielded any suspicious purchases or activities. After which she'd lain awake agonizing over what was worse—being dumped for another woman, or being dumped for no discernible reason.

A low buzzing noise sounded from next door. She stood and glanced out the kitchen window to see Chev Martinez wielding the pressure washer on the stucco exterior of the house. He had removed his shirt in deference to the late afternoon heat, providing a heart-stuttering view of his powerful chest, glistening from sweat and mist. A red bandanna covered his head, giving him a roguish appearance. His jeans were soaked up to his knees, and water dripped from his elbow as he moved the wand, removing years of grime from the house one swath at a time. The dark outline of the tattoo encompassed the muscle of his thick upper arm.

Gemma's body warmed in forgotten areas. The man was exotic and out of place in this sleepy neighborhood, like an animal who had wandered in from the wilds. The tip of her tongue emerged and whisked away the sheen of perspiration on the rim of her lip. But when he turned his head in her direction, she shrank back from the window, feeling foolish, like a sex-starved housewife ogling the pool boy.

She gave herself a mental shake—this wasn't like her. She wasn't the woman at the cocktail party glancing across the room to catch the eye of a handsome man, the kind of woman who flirted with waiters and shoe salesmen. She had been physically committed to her husband, had closed her mind to the idea of touching another man, or having another man touch her.

She didn't know how to behave like a single woman, couldn't remember the vocabulary, the body language.

Suddenly she felt tired, her lazy muscles taxed from cleaning. She needed to take a shower and start thinking about tomorrow's appointment at the employment office. She pitched the old newspapers and sorted the rest of the mail, tossing Jason's magazines and catalogs into a basket, her fingers hesitating over the divorce decree.

Where did one keep their divorce papers? In a box with

their defunct wedding photos and marriage license? In a file with other routine documents like tax forms and canceled checks? In a frame, mounted on the wall?

She sighed, postponing yet another decision. When her hand touched the white envelope—presumably from Covington Women's College—that Chev Martinez had delivered, a nostalgic pang struck her. She had savored her time at the school, had been ecstatic to escape the suffocation of her parents' close supervision. The young women she'd met there had seemed so much more worldly and more mature than she'd been. Gemma had been content to hover on the periphery of their candid opinions and heated debates about the human condition, trying to soak up their moxie.

She tore open the flap with her thumb and removed the contents, another envelope tucked inside a cover letter. The yellow flowered envelope plucked at a memory chord. On it was written a series of numbers and letters that made up a code of sorts—she frowned—in her own handwriting?

Unfolding the crisp cover letter, she scanned the letterhead. *Dr. Michelle Alexander* elicited another tug on her memory, compelling her to read on to determine why.

Dear Ms. Jacobs,
You were a student in my senior-level class titled
Sexual Psyche at Covington Women's College. You
may or may not recall that one of the optional assign-
ments in the class was for each student to record her
sexual fantasies and seal them in an envelope, to be
mailed to the student in ten years' time. Enclosed you
will find the envelope you submitted, which was care-
fully catalogued by a numbered code for the sake of
anonymity and has remained sealed. It is my hope

*that the contents will prove to be emotionally con-
structive in whatever place and situation you find
yourself ten years later. If you have any questions,
concerns or feedback, do not hesitate to contact me.
With warm regards,
Dr. Michelle Alexander*

Wonder flowered in Gemma's chest as memories came
rushing back in a torrent of disjointed images. The Sexual
Psyche class had been legendary at Covington. Jokingly
dubbed "Sex for Beginners" by the female students, Gemma
had felt naughty simply signing up for it. She recalled how
nervous and self-conscious she'd been the first time she'd
slid into a seat in the rear of the class, eyes lowered.

Dr. Michelle Alexander had been a lush-hipped woman
with long, dark wavy hair and a wide, warm smile. She had
made sex seem like a glorious gift rather than the obligation that Gemma's mother had conveyed. Gemma had been
mesmerized, wondering as the woman lectured on the
virtues of self-gratification and multiple orgasms, how
many lovers she had at her beck and call. The class had been
an awakening for Gemma, an outlet for all the pent-up
questions she had about a topic that had long mystified her.

She fingered the flowered envelope, oddly embarrassed
at the prospect of reading things she'd written as a virgin,
before she'd even met Jason, now that she thought about
the timing.

Gemma bit into her lip. Why was the prospect of having
insight into the woman she'd been before Jason so unset-
tling? After all, she had come full circle.

4

GEMMA CARRIED the envelope upstairs along with a half bottle of wine, deciding to take a shower and relax before delving into the past. The air on the second floor was warm and moist. She glanced at the clock and groaned—she'd forgotten to call a service company to come fix the air conditioner. Tonight was going to be a hot one.

But the water in the shower was cool. She slipped beneath the stream and leaned her head back, capturing a mouthful of water, then expelling it straight up. She smiled, realizing she hadn't done that in a while. It was such a silly thing to encourage her, but it did. A unwitting moment of pleasure, a few seconds of forgetfulness.

Then she spotted one of Jason's razors in the shower caddy, and the awful feeling, which she imagined as similar to being in a car accident, returned. No warning, no control and no mercy. And the numbness afterward, the deep denial that something that happened countless times a day to other people could happen to her. She and Jason—they had been special…different…happy.

Wrong, wrong, wrong.

She soaped and rinsed her skin hurriedly, suddenly eager to get out of the shower, to stop her mind from wandering to unhealthy places. When she turned off the water, she picked up Jason's razor and tossed it in the garbage can. Then she pulled a towel from the rack to blot her hair and pat her skin dry. She caught a glimpse of herself in the mirror and stopped for a candid appraisal.

Out of neglect, her hair was a little longer than she normally kept it, but it made her look younger, softer. She had always taken care of her body through Pilates and regular outdoor activity, and although she might have lost some definition over the past few weeks of apathy, she still looked as good naked as she ever had.

She ran her hands over her breasts and down her flat stomach.

Had Jason simply grown bored with her? She turned to look at her behind, wryly checking for an expiration date she might have missed. She was no longer a coed, but she refused to believe she was past her prime.

Gemma wrapped a towel around her and tucked the ends between her breasts, then padded to the bedroom. After splashing a hefty portion of red zinfandel into a glass, she settled into an oversize chair and picked up the yellow flowered envelope. She held it for a moment, trying to remember the contents. She closed her eyes and visualized the dorm room she had shared with Sue and two other girls her senior year. She'd kept her stationery in a box under her bed. A memory flickered and she recalled that she'd sat up with a flashlight to work on the assignment— the act of writing down her sexual fantasies in the daylight had seemed unthinkable.

Two mouthfuls of the wine made a mellow path down her throat. She carefully worked loose the old, dry adhesive on the envelope, her heart quickening behind her breast-bone. Removing several neatly folded stationery sheets, she recognized her girlish handwriting—more timid back then, tighter, smaller.

The subject matter probably had something to do with that, she conceded.

The date was January, the last semester of her senior year.

I don't know how to start this letter, really. The instructor of our Sex for Beginners class says we're supposed to write down our sexual fantasies. Dr. Alexander says that we'll learn a lot about ourselves by understanding our deepest desires. In ten years, she's supposed to find us and send us our letters. In ten years I'll be thirty-two and it seems so far away I can't imagine what I'll be like then.

Gemma released a dry laugh. Ten years had evaporated, and she still didn't have a clue as to who she was.

And as far as the sexual fantasies go, I'm not sure I know enough about sex to know what excites me. You see, I'm a virgin, so I don't know what it feels like to make love. I've never even seen a naked man, except for pictures. And I watched a couple of X-rated videos with Sue that she got from some guy. Sue says that sex is more fun for the man than the woman and that doesn't seem fair. The women on the porn video seemed to be having fun, though.

I touched a penis once, at a party. The guy was kissing me and shoved my hand down his pants. It was softer than I thought it would be, and hairy. Then he came in my hand and I had to go to the

*bathroom to wash it off. It smelled strange and not
at all like I thought it would. When I came out of the
bathroom, the guy acted like he didn't know me.*

Gemma grimaced. She didn't remember the guy, but she
remembered the incident. How naive she'd been.

*I didn't really care because I didn't like the guy. But
there was another time, another party, another guy.
He just looked at me from across the room. We never
talked and he didn't touch me, but there was something about the way he watched me that made me
tingle all over. It made me wish I was wearing something sexy. It made me want to touch myself in front
of him. It made me feel like I was someone else.*

So I decided to become someone else.

Gemma stood abruptly, taking a deep drink from her
glass, unwilling to read further—at least for now. Her sex
vibrated on a low hum, her pulse hammered. Blocked
memories came flying back….

Dr. Alexander had not only encouraged her students
to write down their fantasies, but to act them out in a safe
way. The idea had captivated Gemma, who had always
kept her emotions bottled, ignoring an itch she couldn't
identify. The assignment was a permission slip to mis-
behave. For a week she had played the role of an exhibitionist, donning disguises and leaving campus to act
out her fantasies.

The things she'd done made her face burn even now. And
she'd come very close to getting into serious trouble. The experience had scared her straight, so to speak. And a few

weeks later, she'd met Jason, and her life had fallen into place. She'd been so grateful to have escaped that little detour unscathed. No wonder she hadn't been able to recall what she'd written—because it was better left unremembered.

Hastily refolding the letter, she returned it to the envelope. She paced, now restless, her mind racing. It was silly to rehash schoolgirl fantasies anyway. They had nothing to do with the current state of her life.

The phone rang, breaking into her erratic thoughts. She glanced at the caller ID screen, praying it wasn't her mother. It was Sue.

The lesser of the two evils.

Gemma picked up the receiver. "Hello."

"Hi, just thought I'd check in. How was your day?"

"I got the final divorce papers today."

"I'm so sorry, Gemma."

"As if it's your fault."

"Have you heard from Jason?"

She pushed her hand into her damp hair. "No. The doorbell rang this morning and, like a fool, I thought it was him."

"Who was it?"

"Some guy who's fixing up the house next door."

"Some guy? Is he cute?"

Gemma thought of Chev Martinez's sexy eyes and calendar body. "I really didn't notice."

"What did he want?"

"He was just delivering a piece of my mail that he found. Hey," she said to change the subject, "I have an interview tomorrow with an employment agency."

"That's great! Are you excited?"

"Yeah, I'm actually looking forward to it. Oh, and I talked to my mom today."

"How'd that go?"

"It was a disaster of monumental proportions. Basically, she assumes the divorce is my fault, that I didn't keep Jason happy in bed."

"Oh my God, your mother actually said that?"

"Yes. Hearing my mother talk about sex was like listening to a frequency not meant for humans. I think my eardrums might have burst."

Sue laughed. "Well, at least you're starting to sound like yourself again. Your mom will come around. They were just blindsided, that's all."

"Weren't we all?" Gemma said. "I also had two phone messages from reporters asking me to comment on the divorce."

"I'm not surprised. Did you call them back?"

"Of course not. One of them was that toad Lewis Wilcox who so blatantly opposed Jason's election."

"Nice of you to protect Jason, considering."

Gemma pressed her lips together—old habits were hard to break. "It's not just to protect Jason. I don't want the attention, either. Besides, it's not as if I have any sordid details to divulge."

"But it's just the kind of thing that Jason's political opponents would love to turn into a scandal if they could."

"The funny thing is, the truth is too boring for a headline: State Attorney General Tells Wife, 'I'm Just Not That Into You.'"

Sue laughed. "At least now that the divorce is official— and public—it'll be easier for you to move on."

"As if I have a choice."

"Things are going to be fine, I promise."

Gemma sighed. "I know. I just want it to be sooner rather than later."

"Call me tomorrow after your interview to let me know how it went."

"Okay, bye."

Gemma returned the phone to its cradle, feeling a surge of appreciation for Sue who had better things to do than make sure her newly divorced friend was treading water.

Sue was right…things were bound to get easier. A job would help Gemma find a center for her new life and leave her less time to dwell on her failed marriage. She glanced at her closet and frowned. She knew how to dress for a fund-raiser, for a luncheon and for a political rally, but what did one wear to a job interview these days? Some companies encouraged their employees to dress casually, while others policed toe cleavage.

When she opened the folding doors of the closet, she nursed a fleeting pang for the empty side Jason's clothes and shoes had once occupied. A few odd hangers, a plastic collar stay, and a dry cleaner's receipt were all that remained. How many times had she wished for more closet space? She had it now, she thought as she spread her clothes across the entire length of the rod.

Flipping through suits, jackets, pants and skirts, Gemma discarded one thing after another as being too staid, too dressy or too casual. Her fingers skimmed over an exquisite black beaded gown she'd worn to a state government function and she wondered wistfully if she'd ever have an opportunity to wear it again. Finally she withdrew a tailored shirtdress and turned toward the mirror, dropping her towel. Then she gasped.

She'd forgotten that she had a new neighbor and could no longer walk around nude in her bedroom.

But at the sight of the darkened window across from hers, she exhaled in relief. Considering the late hour, Chev Martinez had probably left to have dinner or perhaps had collapsed into whatever makeshift bed he'd set up in the house for himself.

Then Gemma pressed her lips together as a deliciously taboo thought, lubricated by the wine, slid into her mind. Just what would she have done if the hard-bodied carpenter *had* been standing at the window, watching?

CHEV STOOD frozen to the floor. He'd come back to the upstairs bedroom to close the window and collect a few tools. Then he'd glanced up in time to see Gemma Jacobs perfectly outlined in her bedroom window as she dropped her towel.

His throat contracted at the sight of her naked body, her breasts heavy, her waist narrow, her hips curved. Her skin was pale and translucent, her nipples pink and puffy. The triangle of hair at the juncture of her thighs was light brown. His cock began to throb, and he was afraid to move, afraid she would hear him or detect movement in the darkened room. He wasn't a Peeping Tom, yet he couldn't bring himself to look away. He'd fantasized about her too often…having the chance to observe her, unseen, was too much to resist. She was unaware he was watching. He was only hurting himself, he reasoned.

Gemma was looking into a mirror and holding up a blue dress, a nice color for her. She laid the dress on the bed and, from a drawer, withdrew bra and panties. When she leaned over to step into the panties, her breasts fell forward, sending blood rushing away from Chev's brain and to his erection. She pulled the pale pink panties high on her thighs, then reached for the lacy bra. Putting her arms through the straps, she fastened the bra with a front closure, then arranged her breasts in the cups.

Chev swallowed hard. He'd never dreamed that watching a woman put clothes *on* could be so erotic.

She lifted the dress over her head, arching high. He could almost hear the rustle of the fabric as it shimmied down over her body. She buttoned the dress slowly, turning this way and that, then fetched a pair of high-heeled shoes to step into, rendering her long legs even longer, emphasizing the curve of her calves. He thought she looked beautiful, but she made a face, apparently dissatisfied, then proceeded to unbutton the dress with maddening slowness and lift it over her head.

He let out a small groan. Bra, panties, and high heels—God help him.

Next came a slim skirt and prim button-up blouse. "Nice," he murmured, although she wasn't showing enough leg for his taste.

She pirouetted in front of the mirror, then shook her head and, to his delight and despair, undressed again. Her breasts threatened to spill out of the bra as she moved her arms. He squirmed to adjust his erection that now bordered on painful. A bead of sweat trickled down his tense back.

Next came another dress, this one a floral number with a swingy skirt and snug bodice. She changed shoes to strappy high heels and as she turned in the mirror, he grunted in affirmation, then whispered, "Lady, you are gorgeous."

He shifted and accidentally nudged the wet/dry vacuum, which hit a ladder, which fell and took down several boards leaning against the wall, all of it crashing to the floor next to the cot he'd set up to sleep on. If the racket alone wasn't enough to alert his neighbor, a fat flashlight came on when it hit the floor, rolling and sending beams of light around the room like a strobe.

Chev dove on the flashlight, but the switch was broken and it wouldn't turn off. As he scrambled to remove the batteries, he glanced up to find Gemma staring at his window—staring at him. Chev realized with dismay that he was shining a light on his own face.

Busted.

5

AT THE SIGHT of Chev Martinez's face illuminated in the window across from hers, Gemma froze. From the guilty look on his face, it was clear he'd been there for a while, watching her. Watching her dress…and *undress*. The pale pink lace bra and bikini panties she wore left more skin uncovered than not. Several outfits were strewn over the bed.

A hot flush spread over her face and arms as she realized just how much of a show she'd inadvertently given him. And while her mind screamed for her to cry out in alarm, to cover herself and yank the curtain closed, her body seemed unable to comply. Slowly she realized that the inability to move was actually the *unwillingness* to move.

It was as if her wanton thoughts of him watching her had conjured up his image, had drawn him to the window. How could she shriek and flail about when she was the one who'd secretly wanted him to be there, and he was the one who looked stunned and…*trapped?*

It would be less embarrassing for both of them, she decided, if she pretended she didn't see him. So, with her skin warm and tingling, she turned her back and unfastened her bra, then retrieved a nightgown to slide over her head.

After the white filmy fabric fell into place, she turned back to the window and pretended to ignore him, although her nipples had hardened and warmth radiated from her sex. She gathered and rehung the clothes in the closet, all the while wondering if he was still there, and somehow knowing that he was. It occurred to her that even wearing the nightgown, silhouetted in the light and braless, she might as well be topless.

Did he like what he saw, she wondered. Feeling naughty, she turned sideways to give him a good view of her profile. Desire blazed through her body with an intensity that she hadn't felt in years…since college. She yearned to touch herself, but she had to remember that she and Chev Martinez would likely be crossing paths again soon. Performing for strangers as she had in college had been risky enough, but performing for a man who knew where she lived…

With slow reluctance, Gemma reached for the light switch and flipped off the bedroom light. Then she crawled into bed and lay there in the still, warm air, her body covered in a sheen of perspiration, pulsing with need. What had come over her? Was this the person she was without Jason? Libidinous? Out of control? Did she need his steadfastness to keep herself morally in check? Was she bound to slip back into the wickedness of her deviant sexual fantasies?

Several minutes later, the sound of an engine starting next door came through the open window, followed by the clatter of his truck leaving the property. She wondered what the dark-haired, dark-eyed man thought of her. Did he think she was depraved, or had she given him a hard-on? If the facilities in his house weren't yet functioning, he might be sleeping elsewhere. Was he fleeing to a girlfriend or wife nearby to share what had happened with a laugh before tumbling into bed? He hadn't been wearing a wedding ring, but that didn't necessarily mean anything, considering he worked with his hands all day.

Night sounds floated into the stillness of her room. Cicadas and other nocturnal insects emitted strident noises in rounds that swelled and ebbed. The perfume of fresh-cut grass and moon-blooming flowers rode the air. She felt utterly alone with her thoughts and nervous about this sense of restlessness her note to herself had reawakened. Knowing that sleep was long in coming, Gemma turned on the night-stand lamp and gingerly reached for the folded sheets of the abandoned letter.

With her heart pounding, she picked up reading where she'd left off, where the unknown boy at a party had watched her from across the room.

It made me feel like I was someone else. So I decided to become someone else. The next day I put on the sexiest pair of panties that I owned (pink with white lace), along with a short pleated plaid skirt and a white blouse. In the bathroom at the train station I put on a brown wig that my roommate had worn in a play, and large dark sunglasses. Then I got on a train going to a part of town where I knew no one. It was rush hour and the train was crowded, but I waited for just the right person. He got on a few stops later. He was cute and wore a gray pinstripe suit. He looked as if he was just out of college, probably working at his first job in an office somewhere. He sat a few feet away, facing me. He noticed my legs first. I was wearing white socks that came up to my knees, and black Mary Jane shoes. His gaze stopped again at my skirt, so I twisted in my seat to lift it a few more inches. And I parted my legs.

His eyes widened slightly and he glanced up to my face. But I kept my head slightly turned. With my dark glasses, he couldn't tell that I was looking at him out of the corner of my eye. He wiped his hand across his mouth and looked around to see if anyone else had noticed the panty show, but no one had.

His face turned as pink as my panties, but he kept watching, kept staring at me, sending tremors through my body. I knew he wanted me. I felt myself grow warm, then wet as I wiggled my skirt higher, my knees wider. I knew I was staining my panties, and wondered if he could tell. Apparently so, because he moved his newspaper over his crotch, then slid his hand beneath it. Knowing that he was secretly jerking off while staring at my pink panties made me feel powerful. I let him get his fill for several minutes, until his eyes went glassy. At the next stop, I got off the train. As the train pulled away, he was craning to see me through the window. I gave him a little wave to let him know that I had been in on it all along.

I could hardly wait to get back to my room. Thank goodness my roommates were gone. I went into the bathroom and closed my eyes, remembering the way that man had looked at me, and I made myself come over and over again.

Gemma set aside the letter, her ears pounding with the thrum of longing coursing through her. She sighed and pushed her sweat-dampened hair away from her face. Her mother's attempt at depicting sex as a necessary evil had backfired. By the time Gemma was finishing up college, she'd been burning up with a curiosity that Dr. Alexander's class had unleashed with a fury. What had been taboo had suddenly seemed accessible, only she hadn't been equipped to deal with the emotional and physical freedom. She'd been young and foolish, tempting fate with strangers in the pursuit of a sexual thrill. It had been liberating and exciting, but she had gone too far.

She was older now, wiser. She could control her fantasies, exercise restraint. She didn't have to act on them like before. The performance at the window had been accidental. She hadn't done anything that couldn't be innocently explained away.

Thank goodness.

Feeling relieved, Gemma turned over her pillow to find a cool spot and willed herself to go to sleep. She needed to be rested for her interview in the morning. Hopefully everything would go well and she would find a job quickly. Then she and Chev Martinez might not have the occasion to even see each other again before he moved on to another job. The incident would be forgotten. Perhaps, it had *already* been forgotten by him.

But her body still hummed with memory of his dark eyes on her, and for the first time since Jason's abrupt departure, Gemma fell asleep with the image of another man in her head.

CHEV PUSHED AWAY the remnants of a steak and baked potato and wrapped his hand around the fresh cold beer that the barkeep set in front of him. The any-town bar and grill was busy for a weeknight, with the jukebox blaring and the brews flowing freely between the men, some still garbed in work clothes, and the perpetually half-dressed coeds that populated every town in Florida he'd ever lived in, from Kissimmee to Miami.

"Lived in" was a stretch—more like visited. Moving from one commercial carpentry job to another, scouting for houses to flip in between. He couldn't remember being anywhere for longer than six months in the past five years, since his engagement to Brooke had ended so disastrously. At least he'd learned that his fiancée slept around—and upside down—before they'd said their vows. For the first two years afterward, he'd worked eighteen hours a day to keep the pain at bay, and by then, the frantic work pace simply became a habit. Lingering in one place too long would simply lead to…complications. His mantra was to keep his relationships light…portable…temporary.

And tangle-free. He didn't need to be arrested as a Peeping Tom for spying on the ex-wife of the state attorney general.

Chev shifted uncomfortably on the stool. He hadn't maintained a hard-on this long since high school, but even after a cold shower and a hot meal, he simply couldn't get the image of Gemma Jacobs out of his mind. He'd thought she caught him watching her, but then she had gone on as if nothing had happened, donning a nightgown that was as good as transparent, giving him a gut-clutching view of her full breasts tipping forward as she reached and leaned and stooped before finally turning off the bedroom light.

It was almost as if…

No. He scoffed. A woman like Gemma wouldn't…

Would she?

He pulled his hand down his face, wondering if it were possible that she *had* caught him watching her but hadn't minded. And, in fact, had extended the performance a little longer…

Then he expelled a harsh little laugh. Wishful thinking. Because the only thing hotter than watching her dress and undress in the window would be if she'd *known* he was watching her.

The moisture left his throat as his cock grew harder. He tipped up the beer and shifted again, troubled by the sudden thought that, after meeting Gemma and now having her nude body branded on his brain, there would be only one way to fully sate his appetite.

Unfortunately, that wasn't likely to happen anytime soon. The woman was way out of his league.

He turned his head and saw two pretty young brunettes staring at him over the tops of their drinks. They smiled and waved, twisting their tanned, nubile bodies to best advantage. Arms draped around each other's shoulders, they kissed full on the mouth for his benefit. He set his jaw at the lust that surged through him and considered the double-header diversion. A heartbeat later, he rejected the idea. Another time, he might have been interested, but tomorrow would be a long workday. It was best to call it a night. He gave the women a clipped nod, then tossed money on the bar and downed the rest of his beer before leaving.

He mentally kicked himself all the way back to Petal Lagoon Drive. Those two brunettes could've taken the edge off his libido and taken his mind off the blonde next door.

For a while.

The house next to his fixer-upper was dark when he pulled into the driveway, dimly illuminated by a dusk-to-dawn light on the street. His loud rumbling truck plowed through the quiet of the upscale neighborhood, reminding him that he didn't belong. He cut off the engine and sat listening to the silence of the suburbs, wondering what it would've been like to grow up in such an insular, privileged environment. A yard…trees…a pool…good schools for him and his siblings…good jobs for his parents. A world away from el Barrio where he'd spent his youth in Miami.

He climbed out of the truck and closed the door as quietly as possible, glancing up at the darkened window of Gemma's bedroom and feeling like a fool. The "performance" had been a fluke, and he'd have to put it out of his mind until the renovations on the Spanish house were done and he could sell it. Then, as far as Gemma Jacobs was concerned, out of sight was out of mind. In fact, starting tomorrow, he would do everything in his power to make sure that he and the blonde divorcée didn't cross paths again.

Staying away from her bedroom window would require a tad more willpower, but he'd put up a drop cloth, shutter the window, blindfold himself if necessary. Just because he hadn't been caught this time didn't mean he'd be so lucky next time.

And just like that, he was already fantasizing about next time….

6

DESPITE AN UNEXPECTEDLY good night's sleep, Gemma was jumpy as she sipped morning coffee standing at her kitchen window. She couldn't decipher if she was most nervous about the interview with the employment agency, or the possibility of running into Chev Martinez again after her unwitting peep show the night before.

His silver pickup sat next door in the early morning light, but all was quiet around the property as far as she could tell. She checked her watch—it was still early, but if she left now, she might be able to get away without even having to make eye contact with her neighbor.

She swung her bag to her shoulder and exited to the garage that seemed bare with Jason's car gone and his sports equipment missing from the walls. A black-and-gold monogrammed golf towel lay on the sealed concrete floor. Her heart squeezed as a fresh wave of loss swept over her. Gemma picked up the towel and ran her finger over the elegantly stitched letters, trying to remember who had gotten it for Jason. It didn't matter, she decided, laying it on a shelf. It was just a reminder of all the details in his life that were no longer her concern. She inhaled deeply and turned toward her car, thinking that if she couldn't rewind time to fix her marriage, she wished she could at least fast-forward to the day when things were okay again.

The pencil skirt she wore restricted her movement as she swung into the seat, but she told herself that she'd better get used to dressing up every day if she were going to rejoin the working world. Thank goodness that no one in Florida wore panty hose, but the rest of her outfit made her feel…proper. She was already eager to take it off. When the image of undressing with an audience of one flashed into her mind, she banished the thought. Squeezing the garage door opener on the visor, she started the car engine, poised for a quick escape. If she were lucky, she could postpone her next—undoubtedly awkward—conversation with Chev Martinez indefinitely.

Gemma put the car in Reverse and glanced in the rearview mirror, then slammed on the brakes.

Sitting behind her car, staring back at her was a large blue fowl, about three feet tall, with a sleek, pear-shaped body and elongated neck. He lifted his small, elegant head and emitted a loud, singsong call, then unfurled his tail plumage in an enormous, dazzling fan of iridescent greens, blues, aquas and golds, all sparkling in the morning sunshine.

She gasped in delight, having never seen a peacock at such close range. It was an extraordinary creature and rather intimidating in its full extension as it preened. It also appeared to be rooted to the spot.

Gemma backed the car out a few inches, hoping the movement would startle the bird into action, but he maintained his ground. She bit her lip and looked around. All was quiet. Nothing and no one around to distract the bird away from her driveway. She lightly tapped the car horn, but the cock merely bobbed his head, sending a plume of brilliantly colored feathers dancing. Gemma put the car into Park, and opened the door to step out.

"Shoo!" She waved her arms and walked toward it. "Go away!"

The creature seemed entirely unfazed.

"Move, birdie!" she shouted, flapping her arms. "I have to be somewhere important!"

The bird extended its neck and hissed at her. Gemma shrank back. She'd heard that peacocks could be aggressive and didn't relish being flogged.

Now what?

A low, rolling laugh reached her ears. She turned her head to see Chev standing at the edge of her yard, hands on lean hips, surveying the situation, a grin on his handsome dark face. Her midsection tightened, both at the sight of him in clean worn jeans and T-shirt, and at the knowledge that he'd seen enough of her last night to play connect the freckles. How would he react to her having ignored him? Would he assume she hadn't noticed she was being watched, or would he assume that she'd noticed and that she'd enjoyed it?

Gemma's face warmed. God help her, she *had* enjoyed it.

He walked closer, assaulting her senses. Her chest rose, pulling at the breast button of her starched white shirt. Her breath quickened and she couldn't tear her gaze from his dark, probing eyes.

"Trouble?" he asked mildly. The tiny gold earring in his left lobe glinted against his bronze skin.

She gestured toward the bird, feeling foolish. "I opened the garage door and he—it—was there. I don't suppose it's yours?"

His smile revealed white teeth and pushed his cheekbones higher. "No. It might have flown away from a zoo, but most peafowl are wild." He looked up into the trees. "Normally they don't travel alone. This fella must be lost from his bevy, or is looking for a new one."

Gemma relaxed a millimeter. "You seem to know a lot about peacocks."

He shrugged, displacing muscle under his T-shirt. "My grandparents used to have some on their property in Puerto Rico."

The exotic lineage suited him. "Does that mean you know how to get them to move?"

He laughed, a pleasing rumble, then strode toward the bird, waving his long brown arms. The bird, apparently more intimidated by someone larger and moving faster, startled, then moved away with a ruffle of bright feathers and a protesting yelp.

"Thank you," she murmured.

"Glad to help," he said with a slow nod.

Was it her imagination, or did his gaze pass over her? Had he remembered her outfit from the previous night's dress rehearsal? Her thighs tingled and she was glad to have the car between her and this enigmatic man who could set her skin on fire with his searing glance.

His mouth opened slightly and she sensed he wanted to say something, but his words fell silent on the heavy, humid air that hung between them. She knew how he felt—words would change everything. An apology would only multiply the awkwardness…a compliment could seem…unseemly.

"I'd better go," she said. "I'm late for a job interview."

His expression cleared and he stepped back with a little wave. "Good luck."

She swung back into the car and eased out of the driveway, glancing in the rearview mirror as she drove away. The man was striding back to his property, head up. Gemma shivered in the heat and exhaled a pent-up breath, trying to steer her mind away from her sexy—and temporary—neighbor and back to the task at hand: getting a job.

FROM THE OUTSIDE, the employment agency looked less than promising, wedged into a storefront in a shabby strip mall between a sandwich shop and a check-cashing joint. She hesitated before pushing open the door but forced herself to keep moving. The middle-aged woman behind the piled-high desk was on the phone, but waved for Gemma to come in. Her sharp, appraising glance left Gemma feeling as if she'd missed the mark with her prim outfit.

"You scare off everyone I send over there," the woman barked into the mouthpiece. "Up the hourly rate and I'll see what I can do." She banged down the phone, then turned toward Gemma. "What can I do for you?"

Gemma considered saying she was at the wrong address, but the image of the bills accumulating on her kitchen table was a stark reminder that she'd already put off this day for too long. "I'm Gemma Wh—er, Jacobs. I have an appointment."

The woman jammed on reading glasses and consulted a large wall calendar. "Yeah, there you are." She gave Gemma a flat smile. "I'm Jean Pruett. Have a seat, honey."

Gemma glanced at the mismatched chair opposite the desk that was filled with stacks of papers.

"Just set those on the floor."

She did, then lowered herself onto the edge of the chair.

"So, what kind of work are you looking for?" Jean asked without preamble.

"Preferably something in the art field. My degree is in art history."

Jean winced. "What's your work experience?"

Gemma shifted in the stiff chair. "In college I was in work-study programs with local museums—cataloguing and preservation."

"I meant lately."

"Oh. Lately I've been involved in charity work mostly, fund-raising, that sort of thing."

"I see. Do you have computer skills?"

Gemma brightened. "I have a computer at home." A castoff from Jason, which she'd never turned on.

"Do you know how to work with spreadsheets, databases or Web design programs?"

"Er…no."

"Do you have a teaching certificate?"

"No."

"Speak a second language?"

"I took a Spanish class…in high school." Which only made her think of Chev Martinez. *Por dios,* the man had a body. But for the life of her, she couldn't recall any other words in Spanish.

Jean sighed. "I'm sorry, Miss Jacobs, but unless you can give me something more concrete, I'm afraid I don't have anything for you."

Gemma felt the flutter of panic in her stomach. She didn't want to rely on Sue or Jason's contacts to find employment. "Surely there must be something."

"Most of the jobs I fill are temporary, either short-term or a few days here and there. They require either specific qualifications, or no qualifications at all, meaning the jobs aren't very desirable. And I can see from your appearance—"

"Try me," Gemma said.

Jean looked dubious, but turned to her computer and clicked on the keyboard for several long minutes. "Something in the art field, you say?"

"Do you have an opening?"

Jean named the art museum that Gemma had called the previous day about the executive assistant position. "They're looking for tour guides—"

"I'll take it."

Jean pursed her mouth. "It does pay pretty well for a part-time position. And it says chances are good it will become full-time. Can you start today?"

"Absolutely."

"Good. Um, there's only one catch…."

7

"A SEX EXHIBIT?" Sue asked with a laugh.

"The History of Sex," Gemma corrected into her cell phone. She checked her side mirrors, feeling self-conscious, as if someone might have witnessed her debut tour and be following her home. Thank goodness the employment agency had promised that her personal information would remain confidential, and she didn't have to wear a name tag.

"Do I even want to know what's on display?" Sue asked.

"Let's just say that no one under the age of twenty-one is admitted. And the tours are by reservation only."

"Ooh, sounds intriguing. Do you get to play show-and-tell?"

"Uh…that's one way to put it, I suppose."

"What aren't you telling me?"

Gemma sighed. "There are…costumes."

"Costumes? You mean uniforms, like flight attendants?"

"Only if the flight attendants work for Incognito Playboy Airlines."

"Oh? Do tell."

Gemma squirmed. "The guides have to wear sexy costumes."

Silence. Then, "Well, you certainly have the figure for it."

"And Lone Ranger masks."

Silence again, followed by, "But that could be a good thing, yes?"

"Considering that I'd rather not be recognized as the ex-wife of the state attorney general, yeah. Jason would be mortified if this got out. The press would crucify him."

"I don't plan to tell anyone," Sue said. "Do you?"

"No." Gemma worked to keep her voice casual. "Have you talked to him?"

"As a matter of fact, I ran into him today in the lobby of the capitol building."

Gemma closed her eyes, hating herself for caring but unable to resist asking, "How is he?"

"Fine. He's fine, Gemma."

In the awkward pause that followed, Gemma sensed that Sue wasn't being honest with her. Had Jason met someone else? Or had there been someone else all along?

"Have you seen your new neighbor lately?" Sue asked in a blatant attempt to change the subject.

Gemma's thighs warmed as the image of Chev slid into her mind. She spoke carefully. "I saw him this morning as I was leaving. He chased away a peacock that was blocking my driveway."

"A peacock? Where on earth did that come from?"

"I have no idea. Chev says they're wild."

"Chev?"

"Er, that's his name. Chev Martinez."

"Sounds exotic. Is he Mexican?"

"Puerto Rican, I believe he said."

"I had a Latin lover once," Sue said with a sigh. "He was heavenly in bed."

Gemma squirmed. "That's nice. And completely irrelevant to this conversation."

"I'm just saying."

"I'm not ready to move on," Gemma said. "You know that Jason is the only man I've ever been with."

"All the more reason to have a fling," Sue insisted. "Gemma, you and Jason are divorced. You don't owe him any loyalty."

"I know. I just don't remember how to be single."

"Be indulgent. Try on new things...new men."

Just the thought of "trying on" a new man made Gemma panic. She was better at performing at a distance than performing face-to-face.

Why else would her husband have left her?

"Right now I'm more worried about trying to pay the bills," Gemma said, derailing the conversation.

"I can still make those phone calls on your behalf."

"I'm hoping this tour guide gig will lead to a full-time job in the museum with a little more...coverage. If it doesn't, I'll take you up on your offer."

"Okay. Gotta run. Talk to you soon."

Gemma disconnected the call and shifted in her seat, staring at the long line of cars in front of her in the falling dusk. She tapped her finger on the steering wheel to the beat of the tune on the radio, frowning slightly when she realized she was listening to a Latino pop music station. She told herself it had nothing to do with the ethnicity of her next-door neighbor and the attraction simmering between them.

It was the job, that was all. The suggestive outfit that she'd worn all day had her on a slow burn and sensitive to the throb of the exotic music. Her dirty little secret was that deep down, she'd experienced a thrill when she'd learned that flirty costumes were part of her new employment. She could feign consternation with Sue, but the only shameful part of being a tour guide for a naughty exhibit was how much she enjoyed it.

She had reveled in watching the eyes of men—and more than one woman—rove over her breasts and legs as she lectured from index cards about the history of erotica and pinups. Just talking about the taboo of nude photography over history had made her breasts heavy and sent moisture to the juncture of her thighs as she explained the lengths that the photographers and models had gone to—including breaking the law—in order to fulfill their own fantasies and the fantasies of people who would secretly view the shocking, illegal photos. The provocative nature of the exhibit hadn't been lost on the patrons. She had noticed couples touching more as the tour progressed and trading knowing looks as they left.

Gemma tugged at the short skirt that had crept up her thighs. The other tour guides had changed out of their costumes before leaving the museum, but she'd wanted to view herself in the getup at home, and at her leisure. She didn't plan to stop anywhere—she'd drive directly into the garage. No one would see her dressed in early fifties' "pinup girl" black miniskirt, fitted pink blouse, fishnet stockings, and peep-toe black high-heeled shoes. In her lap, she toyed with the crisp lace that added a feminine touch to the provocative black mask. The sensation sent erotic vibrations traveling up her arm.

When she drove by the Spanish-style home, she didn't turn her head, but in her peripheral vision she saw that the silver pickup was there. Willing herself not to react to the fact that Chev Martinez was nearby, she wheeled into her driveway.

But blocking her way was the pesky peacock.

He sat in the center of her driveway, head bobbing and tail sweeping the ground behind him.

"Not you again," she said with a groan. Then she rolled down the window and leaned out. "Shoo! Go away!"

When the bird didn't move, she set her jaw. She'd pull forward slowly. As soon as the bird sensed the heat from her car, surely it would move, simply out of self-preservation. She inched the car forward, wincing when the bird seemed determined to stand its ground. The bird disappeared from her sight beneath the front of her car, then appeared suddenly in front of her windshield in a flurry of flapping wings and honking noises, landing on the hood. Gemma cried out and accidentally sounded the horn, sending the bird into another round of hysterics, its claws gouging long marks into the paint of the blue Volvo.

"You're ruining my car," she screeched out the window. The agitated bird screeched back, then unleashed its tail fan on her, as if to scare her off with its dazzling plumage. Among the tail feathers were multicolored eye-shaped designs, a natural defense against predators, meant to confuse. Gemma's irritation gave way to wonderment—the creature truly was extraordinary.

"Quite a hood ornament you got there."

Gemma closed her eyes briefly in half-dread before turning her head to see Chev standing there, his dark head covered in a red bandanna, his skin and clothing coated with dust, his shirt sweat-stained and clinging to his broad shoulders. His dark eyes sparkled with suppressed laughter.

"Hello," she murmured, for lack of anything else to say.

"I think he likes you," he said with a grin. "Although I can't say that I blame him."

Her cheeks warmed as he walked up to the car. She cursed her decision to wear her costume home. What if she'd been in an accident? Or what if her sexy next-door neighbor happened to see her?

She shifted forward in her seat to hide the fact that she was scantily clad, hoping he couldn't see her in the waning light. "I hate to bother you again, but would you mind chasing him off my car?"

Chev waved his arms, grazing the big bird's feather enough to give it a start. It clambered off the car hood and strutted away, crossing her lawn. Her neighbor leaned over to inspect the scratches in the paint. "I think these can be buffed out."

"Thanks for your help," she said, then pressed the button on the garage door remote.

"Don't mention it."

Gemma pulled into the garage, thinking she'd dodged an embarrassing bullet, then realized that Chev was still standing next to her driveway, as if he wanted to talk to her. Lowering the garage door would be inexcusably rude, especially considering that he'd helped her not once, but twice today. So, swallowing her pride, Gemma opened her car door and stepped out. The black mask tumbled to the garage floor. She crouched to scoop it up. Although she was sure he'd seen it, she held it behind her back like a naughty child.

His gaze scraped her from head to toe, his eyes climbing in unasked questions. She had, after all, been wearing a rather prim outfit when she'd left the house this morning.

"Um, I can explain why I'm dressed like this," she said

as mortification bled through her. To her dismay, her nipples tightened in response to his appraising glance.

"It's really none of my business." He raised his hands, taking a step backward.

"It's for a job," she blurted, then realized that her explanation only made things worse. She smoothed a hand over her short skirt but, too late, realized it was with the hand holding the mask. "I'm a museum guide."

One side of his mouth climbed. "I don't remember seeing any guides dressed like that when I was dragged to museums as a kid."

"It's a, um, special exhibit," she said, crossing her arms across her chest in the glare of the overhead light that came on automatically. Admittedly the gesture seemed rather ridiculous considering how much of her he'd already seen. But being this close to him set her senses on tilt, left her feeling vulnerable as raw desire drummed through her limbs. "Thanks again for helping with the peacock," she said, nodding in the direction the bird had wandered.

"You're welcome. He shouldn't stay for long. He's looking for a mate, so once he realizes there isn't one here, he'll move on until he finds a bevy."

"That's comforting," she said, running her hands up and down her arms.

Silence followed, but electricity pulsed in the air between them.

Finally he broke the quiet with an awkward shift of his feet. "I just wanted to let you know that I'll be finishing some things in the house for a couple more hours."

"Okay."

"On the top floor."

She swallowed. "Okay."

"The electric in the house is spotty, so just because you don't see lights on doesn't mean I'm not there."

She realized what he was telling her—that at any time he might inadvertently see something through her bedroom window that she might not mean him to see. "O…kay." It was a gentlemanly way of letting her know that he'd seen her the night before.

"Not that everything I've seen in your direction isn't spectacular," he said in a low voice, wetting his lips.

Desire stabbed her low and hard. She didn't know how to respond, so she remained silent as heat rolled through her midsection, touching off little firestorms all over her body.

As if afraid he had crossed a line, he started backing away. "By the way, a tile crew is coming tomorrow, so there will be a wet saw operating outside. It might be, um, loud."

"I appreciate you letting me know."

"Hopefully the worst of the noise will be over by the time you come home from, um, work."

She felt humiliated all over again. "It's a temp job. I might get called in, I might not." Depending on how many reservations the museum received for the new, untried exhibit.

He nodded to cover what he must be thinking—how sad it was that the job she took not only required her to dress like a prostitute, but that she was basically on call…like a prostitute.

The automatic overhead garage light began to dim. "I should go in," she said.

"Of course. Good night."

"Good night." She waited until he was out of sight before lowering the garage door. She entered the house moving slowly, her underwear displaced and rubbing her in delicate places already tender with engorgement. An unattained orgasm sang low in her belly and she suddenly anticipated a self-stimulated release.

But where, she wondered, glancing around, her excitement mounting. The kitchen table? The shower? The bed? The blast of warm, stale air was a reminder that the air conditioner was still on the blink. She trudged up the stairs, flipping on lights as she went, her stomach growling from hunger. But a deeper hunger stirred in her pelvis.

She walked into her bedroom and turned on the light, then automatically went to open the window to welcome any breeze that might be stirring. As she slid aside the glass panel, her gaze went to the window across from hers. The room behind it was dark. Was he there?

Just because you don't see lights on doesn't mean I'm not there.

But was he the kind of man who would say that, then go upstairs to see what she would do? He'd made it clear that he hadn't looked away when he'd seen her undressing in the window, that he had enjoyed being the unintentional voyeur.

Her heartbeat increased to double time as blood rushed to her breasts and thighs.

Now that they both knew that he'd seen everything, would he scrupulously avoid the window? Or was he standing there, even now, waiting to see what would happen?

CHEV HELD HIS BREATH, hating himself for going straight to the window, but he'd been thinking of little else but Gemma all day, and his desire for her lay smoldering just under the surface. That provocative outfit of hers had been like a match thrown on the carefully banked coals, igniting an instant blaze in his belly.

She stood at the window, her face cast in shadow, her body outlined by the backlighting in her room. Her head was turned in his direction, although he felt certain he was hidden in the inky darkness. She stepped back from the window and he exhaled. She had understood his warning and would take steps to make sure it didn't happen again.

But instead of pulling the sheer curtain across the window, she simply started unbuttoning her blouse.

He stood riveted, because he knew this show was for him, purposely.

Facing him, she unbuttoned the low-cut pink blouse slowly, then shrugged out of it to reveal a black lacy bra that barely restrained her full breasts.

Chev sucked in a sharp breath as his cock hardened behind his zipper. He reached down to massage the length of his erection for some measure of relief. Where was this going, and how far would she take it?

Before the idea had slid out of his mind, he watched incredulously as she pulled the short skirt up around her waist, revealing the fishnet stockings—thigh-highs, Lord have mercy—and minuscule black panties. She lowered herself onto the edge of the bed.

Every muscle in his body tensed. Was she...? She wouldn't, he decided.

But she did.

She slipped her hand inside the black panties and as her fingers found their target, her head lolled backward, her mouth slightly open.

"Jesus," he muttered, dragging his hand across the back of his neck where perspiration had gathered. He knew he should leave for his own good, but he couldn't bring himself to look away. He told himself he would simply watch and not participate, refusing to relieve himself like a horny teenager. So he looked on, dry mouthed and overheated as Gemma's hand moved in a circular motion. He wondered idly how long it had been since she'd had a good orgasm, but he had his answer when, after only a few seconds, her body tensed, then spasmed with her release. His cock jumped in response and he thought he heard the sounds of her cries even through his closed window.

His breathing rasped higher in frustration as he was struck with the urge to ring her doorbell and give the woman a second orgasm the old-fashioned way. She withdrew her hand and leaned back on the bed for a moment, then pushed to her feet slowly and moved to the window. His cock throbbed for release, and he had the crazy thought that she would gesture for him to come over.

She lifted her hand…

And closed the sheer curtain.

8

GEMMA LOVED to make love in the morning…when the young sun suffused the bed with just enough light to see the expression on her lover's face as his body sank into hers. She slid her hand across the bed toward the man from her dreams, then blinked awake when her reach came up empty.

The erotic details of the dreams dissipated like fog, but she was left with the distinct impression of a dark-skinned man and a tiny gold earring. Her back was moist with perspiration, her body still vibrating from the intensity of the fantasies, no longer sated from her self-gratification episode of the night before.

A wicked thrill passed through her at the memory of her wanton behavior, and she wondered if and how her performance had been received. Had he turned away out of dismay, or had he, perhaps, exhausted himself along with her?

The idea of the big man watching her to achieve his own orgasm sent a shudder through her body. Then she bit into her lip—what if he was disgusted instead? What if he had reported her to the police or the neighborhood association as an exhibitionist? Last night when they were talking, she thought she'd sensed his arousal…but what if she'd misjudged mere politeness?

She went to the window and moved the curtain a millimeter. All was quiet next door, with no sign of the silver pickup truck. Perhaps he'd gone to eat, or to pick up supplies.

And then she noticed that the window across from hers was shuttered—the only one as far as she could tell.

Gemma swallowed hard. Was he sending her a message? It would seem so. A hot flush of humiliation scorched her skin as she turned away from the curtains. She'd pushed things too far, had exceeded the boundaries of good taste, or perhaps had trespassed on his obligation to another woman. Regardless, it appeared that he was putting an end to her watch-me games.

With a knot of anxiety in her stomach, Gemma dressed in shorts and T-shirt and descended to the first level. Feeling like a naughty child put in her place, she cursed her carnal weakness and chastised herself for not exhibiting more self-control. And she conceded that while she had considered and dismissed the danger in what she was doing (the risk was part of the thrill, after all), she was even less prepared to deal with outright rejection on the heels of Jason's departure.

Self-condemnation welled in her chest, choking her. God, she was lonely. She glanced at the basket holding Jason's accumulating mail and before she could change her mind, picked up the phone and dialed his cell number. While his phone rang, she reminded herself she had legitimate business to discuss with him and inhaled to compose herself. Should she try to sound perky, or detached? Which, she wondered, would best convey the notion that she'd moved on and was merely tending to the pesky loose ends of her marriage?

Jason answered before she could decide. "Gemma? What's up?" His voice was even and polite, as if he were talking to anyone…or no one.

A sharp pain struck behind her breastbone.

"Gemma? Are you okay?"

His thinly veiled irritation roused her from her wounded daze. "Sure," she said, sounding amazingly normal. "Sorry, I didn't expect you to answer. I was planning to leave you a voice message." She impressed herself with her improvisation.

"What about?"

"Your mail, and some other things you left. What should I do with them?"

"Is it anything important?" He sounded as if he was walking somewhere, juggling the phone.

She hardened her jaw. "Not to me. Some magazines, golf stuff."

"You can toss it as far as I'm concerned. I took everything that meant something to me."

Right between the eyes. She blinked, then nodded. "Okay, then."

"Did you tell your parents yet?" For the first time, she detected a note of sadness in his voice. It made her wonder if he'd prolonged the marriage for their sake.

"Mom called yesterday—she'd heard from another source. Did your office issue a statement?"

"No, we decided it was best just to ignore it and answer questions as they arise."

Ignore it. "I…" She almost faltered. "I have phone messages from several nonprofits asking me to help with their upcoming fund-raisers, on your behalf, of course."

"Divert them to my secretary. She'll take care of it, make appropriate excuses."

She wondered if kind old Margery knew that, after ten years, Jason still referred to her by her position instead of her name. Had he previously treated his wife with similar disrespect when talking to others?

"Is that all?" he asked, clearly already thinking about something else. "Do you need my help with something, Gemma?"

"No," she murmured. "I'm fine."

She hung up the phone quietly, in opposition to the fact that her heart was shattering all over again. She straightened her shoulders and exhaled. She wasn't fine yet, but she was going to work harder at it. Somehow she was going to find herself again, the woman she'd been before meeting Jason.

While she ate a bowl of cereal, she thumbed through the yellow pages for the names of companies to service her air conditioner. The first two she called were three weeks out on appointments, the third could come within a week at a price that took her breath away. She hung up the phone and decided that the sultry indoor temperatures were tolerable after all, at least until she achieved full-time gainful employment.

She checked her watch—8:15 a.m. Jean at the employment agency had said she'd call by eight o'clock if the museum needed Gemma, so it looked as if she needed to make alternate plans for her day. Hopefully by tomorrow, word of mouth about The History of Sex exhibit would have spread and the three newly hired guides would be booked solid.

She sipped the last of her coffee while standing over the sink, sneaking glances next door to see if Chev's truck had appeared. It hadn't. She decided she'd take advantage of the lower morning temps and work in her neglected yard.

She went to the garage and plucked her wide-brimmed straw sun hat from a hook, retrieving the floral garden gloves that she stored inside the crown. She hesitated before putting on the protective gear. The last time she'd worked with her flowers and plants, her life had been bumping along fine…at least, as far as she'd known. Jason had arrived home late, as usual, and she was still thinning the daylilies, having lost track of time. He had been irritated with her, she recalled, because she hadn't started dinner. And even after she'd reported spending most of the day volunteering at a local community center (representing his name and office), he had left her with the distinct feeling that she wasn't living up to her end of the bargain as a political wife, not contributing enough to his happiness.

She had been stunned and hurt, but had attributed it to postelection stress. In hindsight, it had been a warning of what was to come only a few days later.

She donned the hat and gloves, then pulled the lawn mower from the corner and gathered her bucket of gardening tools. A narrow door in the rear led to the backyard and patio. The wrought-iron table and chairs, with floral pillows and matching umbrella had been left by the previous owners and Gemma imagined a happy couple sitting there having an evening cocktail and winding down from the day. On occasion, she had brought reading materials out here to enjoy under the shade of the umbrella, but she couldn't recall Jason ever joining her.

As she picked up the festive pillows to rid them of leaves and debris, she wondered if Jason had decided to leave even before they'd bought this house…and then realized with jarring clarity that he probably had. He'd seemed detached throughout the buying and moving process, and other than setting up his office and staking claim to half the closet space and enough room in the garage for his golf equipment, he'd shown very little interest in either the house or the neighborhood. Because he'd known his days there were numbered?

From the patio she could see the back of the Spanish-mission-styled house next door. The tile walkways were broken and, in some places, missing altogether, and the yard and landscaping were overgrown. But other than a cracked and peeling oval-shaped pool, long since drained, the house itself looked to be in better shape from this side. She idly wondered what color Chev planned to paint the house and if he planned to restore architectural details. Probably not, since he'd made it clear he was flipping the house when it was finished.

The man would be gone within a month, and forgotten.

With a mental shake, she reminded herself that she had too much to do around her own house to be thinking about the goings-on of the man next door. Especially since he had likely dismissed her from his mind.

The grass was deep from neglect, necessitating two passes with the mower, one on a high setting, and one lower to the ground. But the physical exertion felt good, and the aroma of fresh-cut grass never failed to lift her mood. Before long, the tiny back and side yards were neatly shorn, and she had worked up both a sweat and a powerful thirst.

Retreating to the relatively cooler temperatures of the kitchen, she wet a paper towel and dabbed at her forehead and neck. From the refrigerator she retrieved a bottle of tea. Hearing a vehicle arriving next door, she glanced out the window over the sink to see a large flatbed truck back onto her neighbor's property. Its cargo appeared to be columns— many of them, in different shapes and sizes. The driver sounded his horn, then jumped down from the cab. When

Chev Martinez didn't appear, the driver gamboled to the door but still received no answer. He returned to the truck and appeared to check a clipboard against information stamped on the bottom of the columns. After much head-scratching, he looked utterly confused.

Finally, he set aside the clipboard and unloaded a column that caused Gemma to frown—it was clearly Corinthian, probably not the style that Chev had ordered to replace the ones that had once supported the arched entry porch. After a few seconds' hesitation, she went outside and walked next door, signaling the driver.

"Maybe I can help?"

"Are you the owner?"

"Uh, no. But I know something about the house, so if you're confused about which columns to leave, I might be able to offer some guidance."

He looked relieved. "That'd be great. If I leave the wrong ones, I can't come back until next week. The numbers are smudged, so it could be any of three different kinds I got here."

Gemma looked over the wood columns stacked on the flatbed like thick slabs of lumber and pointed out the pair that Chev had likely ordered. "The twisted ones."

The man unloaded the columns in a cleared spot alongside the driveway, then came back to where she stood and extended his clipboard. "Will you sign for these, lady?"

She hesitated, suddenly nervous at having made a decision about something that was none of her business. She was saved from responding by the arrival of a silver pickup truck. "Here's the owner now."

Chev pulled up next to the bigger vehicle and swung down from the driver's seat. His gaze swept over Gemma and she was suddenly conscious of her sweat-soaked, stained work clothes. Remembering the shuttered window, her heart thudded in her chest.

"Is there a problem?" Chev asked.

The man pointed to the column he'd first taken off the truck. "Your neighbor here saw me unloading this column." Then he gestured to the pair he'd unloaded. "She said those were probably the ones you ordered instead."

Chev's gaze flitted back to her, molten in his appraisal. "She's right."

"Sign here," the guy said.

Gemma stood there until the driver pulled away, feeling awkward, her vital signs heightened. "I didn't mean to be nosy," she said in a rush. "But the driver looked confused and I was relatively sure you weren't going to install a pair of Corinthian columns on the front of a Mission-style house."

His slow grin melted her apprehension. "You're right. I owe you. That one mistake could've set back the entire project."

She shrugged, ridiculously pleased. "It was nothing. Besides, you've come to my rescue more than once the past couple of days."

He glanced around. "Any sign of our resident peacock?"

"Not today."

"Maybe he's moved on."

She nodded. "Well, I should be getting back to my yard work."

He nodded, but his gaze darkened and his lips parted, as if he wanted to say something…about last night? The tension in the air vibrated between them like a taut wire, but Gemma couldn't bring herself to look away.

"How about taking that tour we talked about?" he asked, nodding towards his place. "Actually, I could use your advice on a couple of other things inside the house since you know about the architecture."

"I'm no expert," she protested, shaking her head.

"Still," he said, coaxing her with a smile.

Between that smile and her burning curiosity to see the inside of the building, Gemma relented. "I'd like that."

He led the way, and she fell into step next to him, a tingle of anticipation in her stomach both at the prospect of seeing the interior of the house and at spending time with the vibrant, exotic man. He was dressed in work clothes that were, at this time of the day, relatively clean. She touched her hair self-consciously. "I must look a fright."

His sexy smile enveloped her in its radiating warmth. "You look great to me."

She blushed and chided herself for sounding coy when last night she'd climaxed in front of him, not caring—hoping, even—that he'd been watching.

He seemed to drag his gaze away from her. "The columns are meant for here, of course," he said, sweeping his arm toward the covered porch, whose roof was being held in place with several planks of wood that had been nailed together as a makeshift support system.

"They'll be perfect," she murmured.

He stopped at the front door. "I should've asked—have you ever been inside?"

"No. But I've peeked through the windows a few times." Then she blanched. Peeking through windows was becoming a theme where the two of them were concerned.

From the way he looked at her, she knew that he'd noticed her gaffe. Heat suffused her face, but his brown eyes glinted with the light of a banked fire. "It's even better when you can see things up close."

She swallowed hard, unable to maintain eye contact. He opened the door and motioned for her to precede him. When she brushed by him, a jolt of electricity shot up her arm where warm pink skin met warm brown skin. Warning bells sounded in her head. If the man could ignite her essence with an accidental touch, what kind of sensual assault could he perpetrate on her with full body-on-body contact?

Dismissing the thought with a mental shake, she walked into a once-grand foyer that even in its state of decay, served up a soaring welcome, from the wrought-iron chandelier to the curved staircase that led to the second floor. Terra-cotta tile at their feet, much of it now cracked and dull from dirt and age, stretched in both directions.

"Wonderful," she breathed.

"I'm going to have to replace most of the tile inside and out," he said ruefully, then led her to the left into a long kitchen/keeping room.

"It's huge," she observed. And it wasn't hard to imagine a family gathered here, laughing and passing heaping platters of food. Regret pinged through her chest. The holidays this year would be an awkward, lonely affair with only her and her frosty parents.

"I'd like to put in oversize appliances," he said. "What do you think?"

Gemma's eyebrows climbed. "About appliances?"

He shifted from foot to foot. "From a woman's point of view. It's been my experience that the kitchen usually makes or breaks the sale."

She hesitated. "Well, I'm not much of a cook…lately. But I'd say anyone who recognizes what a great kitchen this is will want appliances to measure up. Personally, I'd love a firebrick oven." She turned her head and smiled at the colorful picture that, with an inset wood frame, appeared to be built into the wall. "A mural, how lovely."

He made a mournful noise as he fingered the worn, moldy piece of canvas. "Unfortunately, it's so deteriorated I'm going to have to tear it out and fill in this area of the wall."

"That's too bad," she murmured, then turned to the end of the room. "Look at the fantastic natural light." She walked to the windows that faced out onto the dry, cracked pool in the backyard. "Are you going to restore the pool?"

He nodded. "I'm going to have it retiled."

He showed her two rooms that could be bedrooms, one of which he'd turned into a makeshift office with a card table and a folding chair. A box of files and a legal pad of paper sat on the table, with stacks of product brochures scattered all over. She noted the stark contrast of this man's workspace compared to Jason's home office, which had to be furnished with the best of everything before he could even inhabit the space.

"Do you have another home nearby?" she asked.

"Another home?"

"Do you…live in Tampa?"

"Oh. No. I move around a lot for commercial carpentry jobs. The reason I have so little time to flip this house is because I have a job lined up in Miami in a few weeks."

Why did the thought of him leaving plant a seed of worry in her stomach? She studied Chev's unyielding profile as he led her up the circular staircase. His strong nose, his high cheekbones, his chisled jaw. He exuded power…and sex appeal.

"Some of the woodwork is in bad shape," he said, shaking the wooden banister and watching splintered chunks fall to the floor below.

"Plaster ceilings," she exclaimed, glancing up at the fissures around the iron light fixture.

"Expensive to repair, but worth it, I think."

"Do you already have interested buyers?"

"An auction date is set, and several agents have said they'll have clients here. Assuming I can do justice to the original architecture, of course. She was a beauty."

Gemma murmured her agreement, especially when the second story opened into a master suite and bath that even in its state of disrepair, took her breath away. The wood moldings alone were a masterpiece. Her focus went to the cot set up in the corner of the room, then to the shuttered round window that was opposite her bedroom window.

"This is where I sleep," he said unnecessarily. "The bathroom up here is the only one working at the moment."

She nodded, hugging herself against the awkwardness that seemed to swamp the stuffy room. Wondering what was going through his head, she decided, was worse than knowing. "Awfully warm up here to have the window closed, don't you think?"

"I was just trying to give you some privacy," he said mildly. "This window looks into one of your upstairs rooms."

"My bedroom," she confirmed.

He nodded. "I, um, gathered that."

Feeling bold, she asked, "You don't like what you've seen?"

His mouth opened slightly, then his eyes turned smoky and he stepped in front of her. "On the contrary."

He was standing so close, they might as well have been

touching. His full, sensuous mouth was almost familiar to her. She could see the stubble of a patch of whiskers that he'd missed that morning shaving, could smell the lingering scent of his minty shaving cream. His powerful chest rose and fell quickly, his breathing as rapid as hers. He lowered his head and claimed her mouth in a motion so natural she didn't realize it was happening until she felt the shock of his warm tongue thrusting into her mouth.

Gemma moaned and opened her mouth to accommodate him. Her arms slid around his waist as if she were comfortable kissing a virtual stranger. The kiss went from hot to scorching as he pulled her roughly against him, his hands skimming up and down her back. Gemma gave up the kiss to let her head loll back in pure pleasure as his hands explored her body. He groaned in her ear as his erection pressed into her stomach, and he jammed his hand into the warm juncture of her thighs. She squeezed her legs against his fingers, her knees weakening as desire swelled in her midsection.

His hands felt so good on her body...too good—

Her eyes flew open as the reality of where they were headed crashed down around her. This was where touching led...to a dangerous, vulnerable place...much safer to watch, and to be watched...

She stiffened and withdrew from his embrace. "I...can't."

Chev's breath rasped out as he visibly tried to rein in his libido. "I guess I misunderstood."

Gemma started backing away, stumbled, and caught herself before he could get to her. "No, you didn't. But I need to keep things...at a distance."

Before the expression on his face could turn from puzzled to something worse, Gemma turned and fled.

9

CHEV PAUSED in the sweltering midday sun to shout instructions to one of the many tile workers who was replacing the hundreds of broken squares in the driveway. He pulled a bandanna from his back pocket and wiped his brow before tying it around his head. For the hundredth time that day, he glanced toward Gemma's house, wondering if he'd scared her off completely with his advances two days ago. He half hoped he had.

Then he lifted his gaze to his bedroom window that he'd unshuttered to let her know that he was interested in seeing her, even if it was only, as she'd put it, "at a distance." He scoffed at his hypocrisy—he missed seeing her to the point of distraction. Yet he didn't have time for a fling, and she didn't seem to have the heart for it.

Obviously she was still hung up on her ex-husband.

He grimaced, realizing he'd worked up yet another erection that would go wasted unless he went back to the bar tonight and looked for the conjoined brunettes. Gemma Jacobs had made it clear that she had no intention of getting involved with him…so why couldn't he get her and her performances off his mind?

"Chev!"

He turned his head to see a frustrated foreman trying to get his attention. Back to work.

Whatever Gemma was doing, he decided, she certainly wasn't thinking about him.

"ONE OF THE FIRST historically documented instances of a dildo," Gemma told her rapt audience, "is in Ancient Greece. The earliest dildos were made out of natural materials, such as wood or stone, and sold in public market-places. This particular example," she said, pointing to a crude yellowed phallus mounted on a pedestal under glass, "is made from human bone."

"Guess that's where the term 'boner' came from," a guy in the back cracked, eliciting laughs from the large group.

Gemma smiled obligingly and moved on to the next item on the tour. The museum's concerns about how the X-rated exhibit would be received had been laid to rest. Jean from the employment agency had informed her that the adult-only tours were booked solid for the next month.

Gemma had worked eight hours for the past two days and had the blisters on her feet to prove it. But she'd been glad for the work that pushed her body to exhaustion and her mind to distraction. It kept her from dwelling on the fact that Chev's bedroom window had been unshuttered since their encounter…an obvious invitation to resume her watch-me games.

She inhaled deeply, then exhaled slowly to calm her racing pulse. It was the charged air in the museum, she told herself, that had her thinking of Chev and his big, strong hand jammed between her thighs. Behind the mask that shielded her identity from the tour group, perspiration moistened her hairline. Today's crowd was more bawdy than most, tossing around jokes and innuendos that fueled the atmosphere to an almost palpable level. She'd lost a few couples already, slinking away to alcoves in the museum, she supposed, to indulge in a quickie before rejoining the tour.

Gemma used her tongue to whisk away a sheen of perspiration on her upper lip. She was beginning to feel like a fluffer on the set of a porn movie—the person who keeps everyone aroused between takes, but who never gets in on the action. The black corset she wore under a cropped jacket was chafing her nipples, and she ached to free them. But the costume of short shorts and jacket with stilettos was one of the most popular with the attendees—men and women alike were devouring her. Her sex and her breasts were heavy with awareness.

"This apparatus," she said, pointing to a metal device that resembled a bulky thong on a nude female mannequin, "is a chastity belt, which was padlocked to prevent access for sexual intercourse. They were common in the Middle Ages when crusading and wars were widespread. Some women wore them voluntarily to ward off rape, and some wore them to pledge fidelity to their husbands who might be away at war for years at a time. And some were installed by jealous husbands who wanted to ensure their wives would remain faithful during their long absences."

"Looks painful," a woman remarked.

"Which can be its own turn-on," another woman offered slyly.

A chorus of concurring murmurs met uncomfortable laughter as members of the crowd reacted. Gemma waited until the din had died before moving on to the room that housed furniture manufactured for the purpose of aiding sex—swings, contoured chairs, adjustable beds and benches.

Everywhere she looked, she saw Chev, making good use of the devices, his long, brown body poised for a session of Tantric sex. Although she had the feeling that a man like Chev didn't need props to shake a woman to her core. The sheer intensity of his kiss still plucked at her nerve endings.

She moved through the rest of the tour with the scent of his skin in her nostrils, the pressure of his mouth on her lips. By the time she bade the group farewell, she was ready to combust. She slipped into the employee ladies' room, lifted the mask to her forehead, and wet a paper towel to hold against her warm neck. The mirror reflected flushed cheeks, dilated eyes and swollen lips. Gemma felt ripe and moist.

"You'd think they could turn up the air," came a woman's voice from behind her.

Gemma looked up to see a woman with short jet-black hair with a pink streak wearing an outfit similar to her own. "Yes, it's…warm," Gemma murmured.

The woman lifted her mask, revealing sharp cheekbones and violet-colored eyes. "I'm Lillian," she said with a friendly smile.

"Gemma."

"Nice to know you, Gemma." Lillian adjusted the collar of her low-cut blouse. She was a fortyish petite woman with lush curves and trim, shapely legs. "How do you like working here?"

"It's interesting," Gemma said cautiously. It would be unseemly to say that she actually enjoyed the job, enjoyed injecting herself into the naughty museum exhibit.

"Are you married?" Lillian asked, fluffing her hair with well-manicured hands.

Gemma averted her glance. Eventually she would get

used to saying the word "divorced," but for now, it stuck in her throat.

"I just wondered what your husband thought of you taking this job," Lillian said into the pause.

"I'm not married."

"Oh, well, your boyfriend, then."

"I don't have a boyfriend…at the moment."

The woman looked dubious. "Really? Well, if you want one, this is the right job to find one."

Gemma shook her head. "I'd never date someone I met here."

"Smart girl." Lillian checked her lipstick. "It's probably just as well you don't have a boyfriend. My Joey is furious that I'm doing this—he doesn't like other men looking at me. And," she added lightly, "he doesn't understand why I'd want them to look."

Gemma met the woman's knowing gaze in the mirror and swallowed hard. Was her fixation so obvious that the woman could pick up on a kindred spirit? But then again, anyone guiding this particular tour had to enjoy being in the spotlight to some degree. Lillian blinked and whatever Gemma had sensed was gone.

"So, can you believe how popular this exhibit is?"

"It seems to have caught on in a big way."

Lillian laughed. "Guess someone underestimated just how starved people are for a little excitement in their lives."

Gemma tried to laugh in agreement, but she felt exposed, as if the woman was talking about *her*, and her life. Telling her that she was starved for something too, else why would she have taken this job? And why was she consumed, even now, with the thought of undressing for Chev Martinez? It was simple—she was a tease. She found more satisfaction in performing than in making love. Self-condemnation rolled through her chest. What would everyone think of her if they really knew what dark impulses drove her?

From the outside, she looked so normal, but on the inside, she was burning with her sordid secret.

"By the way," Lillian offered, "I heard that, since the museum denied the requests of local TV networks to tape the tour, it's possible a reporter might infiltrate one of the groups."

"Thanks for the heads-up. What are we supposed to do if we suspect someone is a reporter?"

"Watch for cameras and let the director know afterward." Lillian glanced at her watch, then lowered her mask into place. "We're up in two minutes. Ready?"

Nodding, Gemma settled her own mask in place and exited the bathroom, thinking she should have taken the time to adjust her underwear before the next group arrived, yet knowing why she hadn't—the chafing garment rubbing all the right places was keeping her in a heightened sense of arousal. It promised to be a long, stimulating day.

And—if Chev's window was still unshuttered when she arrived home—a long, stimulating night.

Her face burned with shame. What was wrong with her?

WHEN GEMMA PULLED onto her street, she steeled herself, ready to face either the cocky peacock or her hunky neighbor—or both. But all was quiet when she arrived home with dusk already setting on a blistering day. A few lights blazed in the Spanish house next door, so she assumed Chev would be once again burning the midnight oil. The fact that his bedroom window remained unshuttered sent a tremor through her womb. He still wanted to see her. Had he heard her arrive home? Was he waiting for her even now to appear at her window?

She sat in her car in the garage for a few minutes to postpone her decision, loath to go into the stifling house. When she cashed her first paycheck, she'd get the air conditioner repaired. But meanwhile, what was she going to do about the internal heat raging through her body?

Gemma dragged herself inside the house and listened to three messages—one from her mother to call her back, please, one from her credit card company to call them back, please, and one from the newspaper reporter, Lewis Wilcox, to call him back, please. Ignoring them all, she prepared a quick salad from bagged lettuce. All the while, she felt the pull to go upstairs and undress…and be seen. She fought the impulse, and when her attention landed upon the letter that she'd written of her sexual fantasies, she picked up the sheath of folded sheets. What better reminder of how her carnal compulsions had nearly led her to ruin before?

Her heartbeat picked up even as she skimmed the pages to find where she'd left off reading. Performing for the man on the bus in her schoolgirl costume…and loving it.

I was hooked. I learned from Dr. Alexander's lecture this week that I have a fetish called exhibitionism— I enjoy putting my body on exhibit. Which is very strange considering my personality. Most people would say that I'm a good girl, someone happy to remain anonymous and on the fringes of a group. My mother has pounded the idea of what a girl should be into my head: polite, quiet and accommodating. I was always taught that drawing attention to oneself was vulgar and conceited—better to blend in rather than risk ridicule.

But during twenty-two years of being good, nothing has felt as good as my one day of putting myself on display. I already wanted to do it again, couldn't sleep for thinking about it—what I'd wear, where I'd go, who I would entertain.

I kept my roommate's brown wig, and lied when she asked me if I'd seen it. An exhibitionist and a liar—I was getting good at being bad. I dressed in tight, sexy workout clothes underneath my regular clothes, then packed the wig in a gym bag. I took the train across town to a gym that I'd seen advertise free workouts, then pulled on the wig. I filled out the paperwork using a fake name and address, then went into the locker room and removed my street clothes. After adjusting my black short shorts (with no underwear, they felt very naughty) and white jogging bra, I grabbed a towel and walked out into the exercise area. I scanned the men working out for a potential target, and immediately found one in a twenty-something dark-haired guy in a gray sweat-stained T-shirt and blue running shorts.

The way he looked at me made me warm and moist. I walked past him close enough to smell the male scent of him, then got on the treadmill to run and work up a sweat of my own. The wig was hot, but its heaviness made me feel safe. In the mirror I could see the guy watching me while he made his way around the free weight circuit, adding iron plates to the barbells, then pushing his muscles to the limit. We made frequent eye contact in the mirror—his eyes *were so sexy it was like he was devouring me. My shorts rode up from the friction, cutting into my privates and rubbing me in the most wonderful way. He couldn't take his eyes off me.*

An older woman in sweats walked up to him and I realized that he was a trainer, and that she was his client. He pretended to be all business with the woman, but as soon as he got her situated on the stair climber, his eyes found me again. The tip of his tongue came out and curled upward. I knew exactly where he wanted to put that tongue. Tingling all over, I reached for my towel draped over the front of the treadmill, then purposely dropped it on the floor. He said something to the woman, then casually walked over to my treadmill. My heart raced even faster as he approached, his eyes smoldering.

When he crouched to pick up my towel, he lingered, at eye level with my crotch. My running shorts were more like a thong by this time, and my thighs were slick from sweat and my own personal lubrication. At his angle, I was sure he could see the lips of my sex squeezed out of my disappearing shorts. With every step I tightened my core muscles, and with the constant massage of chafing and his full attention on me, I could feel an orgasm rushing to the surface.

When I climaxed, the strain of not breaking stride only made it more powerful. My hip muscles contracted, and my breath gushed out in heaving pants. Only he and I knew what was happening. A shudder went through my body, but I managed to stay upright and moving. As I recovered, I slowed the treadmill to catch my breath. He straightened and slowly extended my towel. When I took it from him, I noticed the erection straining against his shorts. I used the towel to wipe my neck and chest. My white jogging bra had grown nearly transparent from my sweat, and my nipples were outlined clearly for him to see. His mouth opened slightly, but before he could initiate a conversation, I stopped the treadmill and stepped off.

"Thanks," I said, then turned and walked as quickly as I could toward the locker room. He started to follow me, but his client waved to get his attention. He hesitated, then went to her. I dressed hurriedly without showering and left without seeing him again. For days I fantasized about his reaction to me, wondering if he'd tried to find me and was disappointed or intrigued that the personal information I'd listed had led to a dead end. The thought that he might still be thinking about me, the mystery woman, made me feel so sexy and so powerful.

Gemma squeezed her eyes closed against the deluge of memories pouring over her. She had been young and flush with the excitement and newness of her own sex appeal. The world itself had seemed so…alive. And accessible. Even now, her heart beat faster at the memory of her thrilling adventure of experiencing a public orgasm with a private audience.

Her breath quickened and she felt the pull of the upstairs window like a magnet drawing her, a frame for her performance. And Chev wanted to watch…what better situation could she ask for? After all, the man would be there only temporarily. They could…play…and then he'd be gone. No harm done. She pushed to her feet and slowly walked upstairs, her muscles growing more languid with every step.

The upper floor was suffocating. She shed the cropped jacket and tossed it on the bed, then flipped on a ceiling fan to get some air moving. After a few seconds' hesitation, she walked over to slide open the picture window, allowing it to bang against the casing. The light was on in the opposite window, and a few seconds later, Chev appeared in jeans, shirtless.

His hair looked damp, as if he'd just emerged from the shower. His powerful shoulders and arms were outlined perfectly in the round window. She recalled how they had felt around her—dominant and insistent. A shudder went through her and she was glad for the distance. He leaned forward on the sill using both hands, as if to say that he wasn't going anywhere, that he wanted her to know he was watching this time.

A sweet haze of raw desire descended over Gemma. She acknowledged that she was sliding into a trancelike state. She wet her lips, then lifted her fingers to the front hooks of her black corset, and slowly began undoing them.

CHEV GRIPPED the windowsill harder as Gemma removed the corset, exposing inch after inch of luminous skin. Frustration and fascination warred within him as lust surged through his body. The little tease. She'd made it clear that she didn't want any hands-on interaction with him, but watching her through her window wasn't going to satisfy him.

Still, he couldn't bring himself to look away—he'd been

wound tight ever since the heated kiss they'd shared. He hadn't imagined her reaction…she'd enjoyed it as much as he had. But something was holding her back. Was she afraid of him? Considering his bulk and that she knew next to nothing about him, he wouldn't blame her if she was. But somehow, he didn't think that was the case. If she was afraid of him, she wouldn't tantalize him like this. Because if he wanted to be in her house, in her bed, he wouldn't let a few locked doors get in the way.

Chev gave himself a mental shake—he wasn't an animal, or a criminal. But this woman unleashed something primal in him. When the corset fell open to reveal the heavy globes of her breasts and budded pink nipples, he could actually feel his blood warming as it pumped through his body, thickening his cock.

Still wearing the gaping corset, she unzipped the black short shorts and shimmied them down her hips. At the sight of a tiny triangle of red panties, he groaned and leaned into the windowsill harder. The woman was killing him. His cock surged, the head pushing above the low waistline of his briefs. He could feel the sticky pre-cum oozing out, his balls tingling with the itch to relieve the tension that had been building for days. Damn, this little game of hers—look but don't touch—made him feel young again, back to the days when sex had been new and fun and taboo.

The best thing about maturing had been mastering control of his body, to make sure that his partner was as satisfied as he was. But growing up had also dimmed the sheer thrill of sex. For men and women alike, the erotic recklessness of youth seemed to give way to using sex to emotionally manipulate others. So while Gemma's actions were confounding, he had to admit that the woman had put a zing into his already healthy libido that had him distracted every waking hour and most sleeping hours, too.

He found himself smiling during the day for no good reason. Something akin to giddiness arose in him when he heard her car, signaling her arrival home. As Gemma's hand slid beneath the scrap of shiny red fabric, Chev studied her face as that strange sensation once again curled through his chest. The beautiful lines of her features softened as she began to sink into the rhythm of her fingers strumming her soft center. Her mouth opened slightly, her shoulders rolled languidly; her eyes fluttered and closed. Her cheeks were flushed with pure abandon, and a smile played on her lips. She was happy putting on this private show, and he felt flattered that she had singled him out.

Frustrated, he conceded as he smoothed a hand over his rigid erection—a tiny scratch applied to a raging itch—but flattered. And intrigued.

As Gemma's body convulsed in orgasm, Chev hardened his jaw against the urge to stroke himself to climax. Not yet. There was something going on with this woman, something that compelled her to experience such intimacy with such detachment. He was determined to find out what made her tick.

Face-to-face…hand-to-hand…and sex-to-sex.

10

GEMMA LOVED to make love in the morning…when the sounds of the day were awakening: the soft tickle of tree branches brushing the roof…the vibrating hum of insects drinking from dewy grass…the rattling screech of something that sounded like a cross between a wet cat and a woman screaming "Help!"

Her eyes popped open. The inhuman noise seemed to be coming from her front yard. So much for a few extra z's on her day off.

She pulled on a robe and walked to the picture window, but didn't see anything from that vantage point. She did glance at the window opposite hers, but it was empty. Chev had probably been awake for hours, she decided, remembering the way he'd looked in the window last night, watching her…a zing went through her stomach and traveled down her thighs just thinking about it. How lucky to find a sexy man living next door—temporarily—who enjoyed watching her as much as she enjoyed performing.

The screeching noise sounded again, and she had a feeling she knew the source. She walked downstairs and into the living room for a view of the front yard. Then she gasped. Piles of new mulch and several clumps of flowers—roots and all—were scattered over the recently cut lawn. And the culprit stood in the middle of the mess holding a healthy marigold plant in his beak.

"Not my flowers!" Gemma shouted. As if the bird, or anyone else, could hear her. She nearly ran outside, then remembered her robe and pounded back upstairs for a pair of shorts, a T-shirt and sandals. Her mind whirled for some sort of weapon as she rushed downstairs. Desperate, she grabbed an umbrella on the way out the front door.

"Shoo!" she yelled, jogging down the front steps and into the yard, waving the umbrella at the peacock. It flinched, then squawked at her, dropping the mangled plant it had been holding.

"Go away!" she shouted.

The bird took a few steps backward, then shuddered and unfurled his tail in its magnificent fan in an apparent attempt to intimidate her.

Undeterred, Gemma opened the rainbow-colored umbrella and waved it at the destructive beast for a little intimidation of her own.

Low, rumbling laughter sounded. Her stomach tightened before she even turned around to see Chev standing at the edge of their property lines, leaning on a Weed Eater, his T-shirt already sweat-stained although the sun had barely begun its climb. His lopsided grin did funny things to her vital signs. She straightened and pushed a few strands of hair behind her ear, realizing how ridiculous she must look. Then she lifted her chin. "This isn't funny. This... *fowl* destroyed my flower beds!"

He held up his hand in an obvious attempt to stop laughing. "I'm sorry. But you're only making things worse."

Gemma frowned. "How?"

He walked closer and gestured to the colorful umbrella she held. "Now he probably thinks you're a potential mate."

Gemma squinted at the bird, who did indeed seem to be strutting his stuff versus scrambling to get away. She sighed. "Do you have any better ideas for getting rid of him?"

Chev pursed his mouth. "We males can be difficult to get rid of once we see something we like."

Her cheeks warmed as his meaning set in. A tickle of concern curled in her stomach. It was a good thing that Chev's days here were numbered. Otherwise, he might begin to expect more than she was willing to offer.

He lunged at the peacock, waving his arms, and succeeded in driving it into the air. Flying low, the large bird disappeared into a copse of trees several yards away.

"Thank you," Gemma said. "Again."

Chev's eyes twinkled. "You're welcome, but I don't think you've seen the last of him."

Gemma pushed one hand into her hair as she surveyed the damage to her flower beds. To her horror, tears filled her eyes. "I so don't need this hassle."

"Hey, hey," he said, sounding alarmed. He moved closer, touching her arm. "It's nothing that can't be fixed. I can give you a hand."

"That's not necessary," she said, wiping her cheeks hurriedly and pulling away from his disturbing touch. "I'm just feeling sorry for myself. Besides, you have your hands full with your own property."

"Actually, I was hoping I might negotiate some kind of trade."

Gemma swallowed hard. "What did you have in mind?"

A small smile played on his lips for a few seconds, as if he were considering all the pleasurable possibilities.

"Your expertise in return for any handyman work you have around here."

"My expertise in what?"

"My house," he said, jerking his thumb toward the Spanish structure. I want to stay as true to authentic Mission detail as possible, but I'm afraid I'm in over my head. I thought with your background in art history, you might be able to steer me in the right direction."

Gemma crossed her arms and considered his proposal. "For example?"

He shrugged. "Some guidance on the fireplace in the living room, the light fixtures in the bedrooms and things that I haven't even encountered yet."

"I have some reference books on the Mission style," Gemma said, her mind already sifting through options. She recognized a flowering sensation in her chest as pleasure. She couldn't remember the last time anyone had asked for her opinion on anything. Jason had been the resident expert on everything that mattered, she had simply been the attentive sidekick. "Would you like to come inside while I look for them?" she asked.

He nodded, and followed her. Her heart raced as they climbed the steps and crossed the porch. She turned the knob on the door and swung it open. As soon as he crossed the threshold, she regretted asking him inside. She felt guilty and skittish, as if someone might catch them, and found herself practicing explanations in her head. *He's the neighbor…a carpenter…temporary.*

"Nice place," he said, turning his head from side to side.

She saw the house as he might…clean, but dark and cluttered with little piles of Jason's stuff everywhere—the overflowing basket of mail, the milk crate of shoes and belts and crushed ball caps, the laundry basket of office equipment and thick volumes of books on Florida law. "I apologize for the mess—these are my husband's things." She put a hand to her head and gave a little laugh. "I mean my ex-husband. We recently divorced."

He nodded. "So I gathered."

She was embarrassed. She should've gotten rid of everything after her last phone conversation with Jason. The air seemed especially stifling.

"Sorry it's so stuffy in here. My air conditioner is on the blink. I've been keeping all the windows open, but it hasn't helped much."

"It's helped me a great deal," he said, his voice low and amused.

His candor shocked her—and pleased her. It was refreshing to speak honestly about a sexual experience instead of flirting around the edges. "I'm glad you think so," she murmured, and the air between them fairly crackled with static electricity. His dark eyes seemed to pierce her, and behind the blatant physical appreciation, she could sense his mind was racing, trying to figure out why a nice girl like her would be compelled to exhibit herself in such an intimate way. Gemma broke eye contact as a wave of anxiety washed over her. Honesty came with its own price.

"I could take a look at your air conditioner unit if you like," he offered, changing the subject easily.

"I couldn't bother you—"

"I might not even be able to fix it," he interrupted. "But I'd like to do something for you in exchange for your help with the details of the house."

There it was again, the look that said he wanted—*needed*—her help.

"Okay," she relented, then proceeded up the stairs. "The unit is up here in the hall closet if you want to take a look. I'll try to locate my reference books."

He strode to the closet with a casual authority that she admired, a man comfortable with houses and the things in them. Unlike Jason, she mused, who saw the yard work as a chore, the smallest repair around the house an inconvenient waste of time. He would often grumble that he had two college degrees, yet he was expected to know carpentry, too. He was too busy to be bothered, she'd always reasoned, hating to see him spend his precious few hours of free time on tedious tasks. Rather than bringing things to his attention, she would attempt the repair herself or call a repair service, with Jason none the wiser.

On the other hand, her mind whispered, Chev Martinez wasn't the most powerful attorney in Florida, with the ear of the governor, making decisions every day that affected the lives of everyone who lived in the state. If Jason knew what Gemma had been doing, exhibiting her body to a relative stranger, he'd be shocked and disgusted. He'd tell her that she'd gone slumming…that he was glad he had divorced her before he realized the extent of her perversions and perhaps ruined his career. A stone settled in her stomach. The men were too different to compare, she told herself. Besides, she'd had a ten-year relationship with Jason, and had known Chev barely ten days.

Yet his presence in her house had her on edge, his big body seeming to take up the entire hall as he scrutinized the unit and touched a tube here, a wire there. He seemed to fill the house, his male scent crowding the muggy rooms, his thoughtful hum soaking into empty corners, chasing away the loneliness that had pervaded the place since Jason's departure. Gemma allowed her heart to lift faintly and moved into her bedroom to consult her dusty bookshelves.

"I'm going to check your breakers," he called.

"Go ahead," she called back, struck by how domestic they seemed. Pleasure infused her chest—this little exhibitionist fling was exactly what she needed to help her push through the pain of Jason's rejection. She was suddenly very grateful for Chev's presence—and hoped that he didn't press her for…more.

CHEV WAS STRUCK by the domesticity of standing in Gemma's hallway, doing something her husband would've done if he'd been around. Would her ex object to him being here? Probably. He wondered if the guy had had an affair, if Gemma had thrown him out or if he'd left voluntarily. Chev couldn't imagine a woman more exciting than Gemma, but maybe the guy was a jerk…or gay. Or just a prude.

Chev flipped a breaker and glanced around to check that the section of power extinguished matched what was written on the switch's label. He moved through the motions of the routine repair, feeling relatively sure he could get the unit running again with a few replacement parts.

He heard Gemma moving around in her bedroom. Setting his jaw against the hunger that surged in his chest, he walked to the doorway and rapped lightly. His gaze swept past the picture window where she had undressed for him and over her unmade bed before coming to rest on the sight of her standing in front of a bookshelf, thumbing through a hefty volume.

She looked up, then flushed and gestured vaguely toward the tangled sheets. "Excuse the mess. I slept in this morning until the peacock woke me up."

He nodded, swallowing hard to control the reaction of his body to the image of Gemma undressed and lying beneath him on that bed. But his cock was having none of his stall tactics and began to swell against his zipper. She still looked tousled from sleep and he'd bet the sheets were still warm from her hot body. No wonder the air conditioner had blown. "The compressor is working. I think you need a new thermostat."

"That sounds serious," she murmured.

"Not really," he assured her, shifting slightly in an effort to reposition himself more comfortably. "I'll get everything you need on my next trip to the home center."

"I appreciate your help."

He nodded toward the book she held. "I appreciate yours."

She smiled and held up the book. "What do you want to talk about first?"

"The fireplace," he said randomly.

"Let's walk over so I can take a look."

"I'll follow you," he said, partly because he wanted to view her backside, and partly because he wanted to hide his growing erection. She picked up a sketch pad and swept by him in a cloud of feminine scent—fruity shampoo, heady womanliness and earthy sleep aromas. Downstairs he noticed blank spaces on walls and shelves where pictures had been removed and whatnots were missing. Containers of random men's things sat on the floor—her husband's leavings, no doubt. The rooms were clean, but appeared neglected and unused. She seemed eager to get outside, and he wondered if his presence made her nervous—more proof that she preferred distance between them.

They picked their way across her trashed yard. "I'll help you put things back in order," he offered.

"I'll do it later," she said with a wave. "I'm sure you have plenty of other things to keep you busy. Do you have a drop dead date for getting the house done?"

"Three weeks from now," he said. "This week is demolition and getting supplies. The serious work starts next week."

He led her inside the musty house and she went straight to the fireplace, all business. She touched the broken clay bricks as if they were old friends. She asked Chev what he was looking for in the restoration, but he was so distracted by her he could barely think. He loved the way her brow wrinkled when she concentrated, the way she angled her head as she sized up things. He fell back on what little he knew about the Mission style, describing the fireplaces in his grandparents' home. She made notes in her sketchbook, then some simple line drawings. He leaned in close and added his comments, getting caught up in her enthusiasm.

"All of this doesn't seem like much in return for fixing my air conditioner," she said. "So I'd like to offer to replace the mural in the kitchen."

He smiled. "You're an artist, too?"

Suddenly she seemed shy. "Not accomplished by any means, but I think I could paint a passable landscape, if you're willing to let me try."

"I accept," he said happily. A delivery truck pulled into the driveway, horn honking.

Gemma tucked a strand of shimmering blond hair behind her ear. "I guess I'd better get to my yard."

"I'll let you know when I get the thermostat for your HVAC unit," he offered as they walked back to the entrance. "Will you be around tomorrow?"

"I have to work tomorrow."

In yet another provocative outfit? He set his jaw against the images that exploded into his head. "I'll let you know."

She nodded, then turned and walked back to her own yard, seeming lost in thought. Chev spent the rest of the day finding excuses to look out the window or go outside to his truck so he could catch glimpses of her working in her yard, wearing her big hat and flowered gloves. It seemed incongruous that the woman was so...*normal* and yet so...titillating.

He had a feeling she wouldn't appear at her window that night, but it didn't stop him from looking. He gave up around midnight, lying on his cot with perspiration beading on his pent-up body as his mind played images of Gemma over and over. The woman confounded him, affected him like no other woman ever had. His body ached for her. He wanted to tell her that she didn't have to be tentative around him, that he would take whatever she had to offer for the short time he would be there.

But what if her erotic nighttime shows were all that she had to offer? The woman was still suffering from the breakup of her marriage. Maybe the window performances were her way of safely acting out.

Or maybe her behavior had led to the end of her marriage. Lots of couples had bedroom secrets, but the state attorney general's career probably would've been compromised if anyone knew that his wife was an exhibitionist.

On the other hand, Gemma didn't seem the type to...

He groaned in frustration. The woman didn't fit any "type" he'd ever known. Intelligent but unhappy, educated but badly employed, homey but sexy, bold but unsure of herself...complementary and contradictory.

Chev sighed, willing himself to put her out of his mind,

11

"How's the job?" Sue asked.

Gemma held her cell phone between her ear and shoulder while she tied the belt on the lightweight black raincoat she wore over her costume. She unlocked her car door and swung inside, mulling her response. Her body was strung tight after a day of being on exhibit herself. She was looking forward to getting home and taking a long bubble bath. "Fine, I guess. I'm getting accustomed to the routine."

Sue gave a little laugh. "I might have to drive down there and check out your show."

Gemma hesitated, trying to adopt a casual tone. "Sue, do you remember the Sexual Psyche class in college?"

"Sex for Beginners? Sure, I remember. What about it?"

"Did you ever take it?"

"No. I thought I already knew everything—what a joke. But you took it, didn't you?"

"Yeah."

"And what made you think about the class after all these years?"

"I…received something in the mail the other day that… dredged up old memories."

"What?"

"An assignment that we had, to write down our fantasies. Dr. Alexander said she'd mail them to us ten years later."

"Wow, that's kind of cool…isn't it?"

"I guess, but a bit weird. I wrote them before I met Jason."

"Yeah, Gemma, you were an actual person before you met Jason. I was there, remember?"

Gemma blinked at her friend's sarcasm. "What's with the attitude? You introduced us."

A hesitant hum sounded over the line, then Sue said, "I thought you'd go out, have some fun. Honestly, I never dreamed the two of you would get married."

Gemma's mouth opened and closed. "So…you didn't… you don't think that we were a good match?"

"That wasn't for me to decide. But I admit I was surprised when you and Jason got serious."

"You didn't think I was good enough for him?"

"Don't be ridiculous. The two of you just seemed so… different. You were so earthy with your art, and he was already so judicial."

And judgmental, Gemma added silently. Jason had a way of making people feel they needed to be on their best behavior around him. He had been a lifesaver at the time, a reason to rein in her deviant sexual conduct and keep herself in check. She had needed him, and had worked so hard to be what he'd needed in return. "Well, since it didn't last," she said lightly, "I guess you get the prize."

"I didn't mean to hurt your feelings, Gemma." Sue sighed. "I'm just really happy for you that you're moving on."

Gemma leaned her head back on the headrest. "I don't feel like I'm moving on."

"You have a new job."

"It's temporary."

"And how about that neighbor of yours?"

"He's temporary, too. He's flipping the house by the end of the month."

"That old Spanish two-story? Isn't it kind of a wreck?"

Gemma lifted her head. "Yeah, but it's going to be spectacular. Chev is really paying attention to detail."

"Sounds like you are, too."

Gemma realized too late that her voice was elevated, her words rushed and excited. She backpedaled, adopting a casual tone. "He asked for my help on a couple of historical aspects of the house."

"Oh? Well, you know your stuff, so this Chev guy is showing good sense by asking your advice."

"I'm sure he wants to set as high an asking price as possible when it goes up for auction."

"Uh-huh. What kinds of things are you helping him with?"

"Architectural details. And I'm replacing a mural for him."

"You're painting again? That's wonderful! What's he paying you?"

Gemma swallowed. "Actually, it's a trade. He's going to fix my air conditioner."

"Is he now? Gotta love a man who's good with his hands."

"Sue, I'm not sleeping with the guy."

"Are you at least thinking about it?"

Gemma started her car engine. "Oh, look at that—my phone battery is dying, and I need to get home."

"Liar. At least tell me if he lives in Tampa."

"No. Like I said, he's temporary."

"No strings can be a good thing."

"Goodbye, Sue."

Sue sighed. "Goodbye."

Gemma disconnected the call and shook her head. Sue meant well by encouraging her to have a meaningless relationship to help move past Jason's rejection. But her friend would be shocked if she knew what had already transpired between her and her neighbor.

Just like she would've been shocked if Gemma's exhibitionism in college had been exposed. Shocked and ashamed.

On the drive home, Gemma reflected on Sue's comment that she and Jason hadn't been suited for each other. Had other people thought the same thing? Had people whispered that their marriage wouldn't last even as they were standing before the altar taking their vows? Had her desperation to marry Jason been so apparent?

Had Jason sensed it, too? Even though she'd never uttered a word of her subversive urges to exhibit herself, had being her safety chute worn on him?

By the time she pulled onto her street, both the sun and her mood were on the downslide. Chev's property was crowded with vehicles and equipment and workers, most of whom were loading up to leave. She saw him standing shoulders above them, looking like some kind of primitive chief in his bandanna, his torso bare and brown. He turned his head as she drove past and his dark gaze pierced her to the core, suffusing her chest with pleasure as she wheeled into her driveway.

But at the sight of the peacock in her yard, uprooting her newly replanted flowers, those warm, fuzzy feelings were obliterated, and high voltage anger whipped through her.

FROM HIS YARD, Chev saw the peacock and cringed. Considering the way Gemma had slammed her car into Park and come charging out, he wouldn't be surprised if she were about to wring the poor thing's neck.

The bird veered away, emitting its high-pitched mewling noise. Gemma chased it around the yard, windmilling her arms and stomping her feet. In her voluminous black coat, she looked ridiculous, but the peacock must have found her menacing. The bird lunged, flapping its wings and careening wildly to stay a few feet ahead of her.

The men standing around him laughed and made circular motions with their fingers indicating that Gemma was *loco.* Chev smiled and waved them on their way, then stood for a few minutes watching Gemma chase the squawking bird around her yard, laughing to himself.

It was therapeutic, he reasoned, for her to lash out at the bird. The woman had had her life torn apart and was clearly struggling to put the pieces back together. He couldn't blame her for snapping over a few unearthed flowers. The colorful animal was a handy target for her pent-up frustrations.

For the bird's sake, he decided to intervene.

As he walked up behind Gemma, she stopped and leaned over to grasp her knees. She narrowed her eyes at the cock, which had also stopped running and was eyeing her intently. "I wonder how you'd look on a platter," she muttered.

"The meat is supposed to be an aphrodisiac," Chev offered.

She turned and straightened, looking adorably sheepish, her cheeks pink from the exertion.

"Not that I can say firsthand," he added. "Peacocks are protected in most parts of the world, but some cultures still consider the meat a delicacy."

She glared at the bird. "We'd have to catch him first."

As if the bird had heard her, he extended his wings and

flew up into a nearby tree, then called down to them in triumph.

"I guess that's the reason they've been around for centuries," Chev said.

She stamped her foot clad in a chunky black high heel, then groaned when she realized what she'd stepped in.

Chev bent over laughing, then wiped his hand over his mouth. "Sorry."

"I called animal control," she said, indignant, "but they said they didn't have a place to take the bird even if they could capture it. They told me not to feed it, and if it hasn't left in two or three weeks, they would give me the name of a preserve to contact. They said that *I* was encroaching on the *peacock's* habitat."

"Unfortunately, that's true. We all are."

"But why did it pick *my* yard?"

He grinned. "I guess he just liked the look of your grass."

Her cheeks turned a deeper shade of pink. "Do you think he'll ever leave?"

"Eventually his instincts to mate will drive him to move on if he doesn't find what he's looking for."

The humidity in the air between them suddenly became sticky with mutual desire. His sex grew heavy as he imagined what lay beneath the belted raincoat. Considering the black mesh panty hose and high heels, he was sure it was something pretty damn fantastic. Her pale hair was tousled from the impromptu activity. Her mouth and eyes softened and her gaze traveled over his bare shoulders and arms. His chest expanded as he inhaled sharply. She wanted him…but enough to let him near her? He watched while she visibly struggled with her physical response to him. She looked away, and when she looked back, she had regained her composure.

"How's the house coming along?" she asked in a breezy tone.

Chev exhaled. "We made a lot of progress today. I wanted to show you a couple of things if you have time."

She glanced at her own house and he wondered if something had happened today to make her even more skittish of him.

Then she turned back to him and smiled. "Sure. I'm going to let this mess go for now."

"That's not a bad idea," Chev conceded. "Let it ride. You can clean up the yard once he's gone for good."

He said the words lightly, but as soon as they left his mouth he realized that Gemma might be drawing comparisons between him and the pesky peacock.

One delicate eyebrow arched, but otherwise Gemma didn't reveal what was going through that pretty head of hers. "Let me put the car in the garage."

Chev knew he should have offered to let her change clothes first, but honestly, he wanted to keep imagining what she was wearing under the coat. And he was hoping that when she undressed, she'd do it for him.

He bit back a smile as she dodged more bird deposits and sacrificial plants on her way back to the driveway. He glanced up at the peacock staring down from a tree branch and wondered if either one of them would have any luck finding female companionship at 131 Petal Lagoon Drive.

Not if Gemma's subconscious actions were any indication, he noted. Instead of pulling into the middle of the two-car garage, she carefully maneuvered into the rightmost space, leaving room for a phantom car. He wondered if she even realized she was still holding a place in her life for her ex's return.

They walked companionably to his house and she murmured appreciation at the obvious changes—the terra-cotta tiled walkway was newly restored and glistening with sealer. The arched entryway was repaired with the new columns in place and freshly painted. He stopped at an outside spigot to wash his gritty hands and face, then grabbed his work shirt from the handle of a wheelbarrow and shrugged into it, leaving it unbuttoned. He felt Gemma's gaze upon him and welcomed it. If he could affect her senses a fraction of the amount that she affected his, maybe she'd invite him into her bed instead of relegating him to the role of spectator at her erotic shows.

Especially since even her performances had ceased.

Inside, he helped her pick her way across plastic-covered floors. The tile work and wood planks underfoot would be one of the last installations, lest they be marred by machinery and heavy boots. The newly applied plaster on the ceiling in the foyer emanated a pungent but satisfying aroma. At Gemma's urging, Chev had sought out a metal salvage yard and purchased enough sections of wrought-iron railing to replace the crumbling wooden banisters.

"Gorgeous," she breathed.

"I couldn't be happier with the way it turned out," he admitted. "I'm going to replace the wood window shutters with iron detail, too."

At the mention of windows, he thought he detected a stiffening of her shoulders, but she didn't say anything. In the great room, Chev was pleased to see Gemma's face light up at the newly tiled fireplace.

"It's stunning."

"Thanks to you. I wouldn't have chosen these colors or design without your encouragement."

"I'm glad to help," she murmured, and he thought he detected a wistful note in her voice.

"You're good at this," he observed. "Have you considered consulting for a living?"

"Maybe someday," she said, nodding. "I hope I can put my degree to use for something more than being a tour guide."

"How's that going?"

"Um…fine." But he was alerted to the way her hand went to the vee of her coat to absently caress the bare skin there.

"I thought you said this was a part-time job. Haven't you been working almost every day?"

"The exhibit has been more popular than the museum anticipated." Her voice had dropped an octave and suddenly she fanned herself. "It's really warm in here."

"You can take off your coat."

"I…would rather leave it on."

Then it hit him. Gemma's job turned her on…allowed her to be an exhibitionist in plain sight, in the guise of a tour guide.

His cock jumped against his fly. Damn, the woman was killing him. But she seemed nervous, lifting her hair to fan her neck. He noticed that she had a tiny brown beauty mark on the nape of her neck that matched the one at the corner of her mouth. "I won't keep you much longer. I just want to show you the kitchen."

She followed him to the kitchen where a firebrick oven had been installed and mortared, next to shiny stainless steel appliances.

"It's magnificent," she said, clapping her hands like a child. Then her gaze landed on a long farmhouse wood table, the top of which was several inches thick. "Oh my— where did you get this?"

"Another find at the salvage yard. I don't intend to furnish the place, but it seemed perfect for this spot."

"It is," she said, running her hands over the scarred but smooth surface. She lowered herself to one of the two long weathered benches that matched the table, giving him a nice view of her legs in the black mesh hose.

He swallowed a groan.

She smiled up at him. "You could certainly seat a large family around this table."

"Funny you should say that," he said. "My parents and younger sister are coming to Tampa next week. They're visiting colleges. I have an aunt and an uncle who live nearby, and a young cousin. I thought I'd have them all come here for a little party since the kitchen is operational. It'll give my family a chance to see what I'm working on."

"That's nice." She gestured to the long empty wall behind the table. "I'll do my best to have the mural done before then."

"I wasn't worried about that," he said. "The house will still be a long way from being finished. Actually, I was wondering if you'd like to join us?"

Her eyes widened.

"It'll be casual," he assured her. "I'll have food and a cake delivered. Since the part for your air conditioner hasn't arrived, consider it a small thank-you to show my appreciation for all that you've done."

Gemma pushed to her feet. "Fixing my air conditioner will be plenty of thanks." His disappointment must have been evident because she added, "But…I'll think about it and let you know. I should be going."

He followed her to the front door and out onto the

covered entryway, stricken by the overwhelming urge to drag her into his arms. "Gemma."

She turned and looked up at him, her eyes questioning.

Chev stepped toward her and picked up a lock of her hair. "I've missed you at the window."

Her throat worked and her chest rose and fell rapidly. "I...it felt awkward since we've gotten to know each other."

"If I'd known that," he said with a smile, "I would've stayed on this side of my property line."

That made her smile and her tension was replaced with that matter-of-fact sexuality that made him wild for her. "Are you saying you don't want to be friends?"

He stepped closer and lowered his mouth to her ear. "I prefer friends with benefits."

A small sound of wanting came from her throat, but she pulled away. "Like I said, I prefer to keep things at a distance."

"But it's more fun up close." He slowly untied the belt of her coat, revealing a red satin bustier and black pleated short skirt. He groaned and his cock stiffened painfully as he slid his hands inside to caress her waist with his thumbs. "Gemma, don't you feel this...electricity between us?"

She bit her lip and nodded.

"Then why—"

"I can't," she cut in, looking away.

"But you want to."

"It wouldn't help," she said, sounding resigned to whatever demons were plaguing her.

He put his hand under her chin and forced her to look at him. "I want to get next to you, Gemma. Let me."

Her sigh caught in the moist air between them. Raw

longing emanated from her smoky green eyes. She was wavering. He lowered his mouth to hers and captured a moan.

A car horn blasted into the air, suspending the moment. A white Lexus sat in Gemma's driveway. A person alighted, frowning in their direction.

"Oh, dear God," Gemma murmured. "Mother."

12

AT THE SIGHT of her mother standing in her driveway next door, Gemma's knees turned to elastic. Her lips were still warm from Chev's, his hand still on her waist. And even at this distance, she could feel her mother's searing disapproval.

"I have to go," she said, pulling away, fumbling with her belt.

"But—"

"I'll talk to you later."

Without looking back, Gemma walked stiffly toward her mother. Phyllipa Jacobs stood holding a casserole caddy and leaning against her car as if she might need it to support her weight. Gemma waved in an attempt to diffuse the openmouthed expression on her mother's face.

"Mother…what a surprise." She reached forward for an embrace, but her mother remained immobile.

"Gemma, *who* is that man? Were you…*kissing* him?"

Gemma caught her mother's arm and guided her toward the front door. "His name is Chev, and he's fixing up the house next door. I'm…helping him."

Her mother allowed herself to be hauled up the stairs and onto the porch. "Helping him do what?"

"Choose architectural details for the renovation."

"I came to visit because I'm worried about you, and I find you—" she lowered her voice to a harsh whisper "—in the arms of a strange man?"

"We were just talking, Mother." Gemma worked the key in the lock furiously and pushed open the door.

"What on earth happened to your yard?"

"There's a rogue peacock in the neighborhood."

"A rogue...what? Gemma, have you been drinking?"

She sighed. "No, Mother." But she sure could use a tall one right about now.

After they entered the house, Gemma flipped on lights strategically, once again wishing she'd taken the time to throw out all the items that Jason had said he didn't want. Now they mocked her, proof of her reluctance to let him go long after he'd made it clear he wanted nothing from her.

"It's awfully stuffy in here," Phyllipa remarked.

"The air conditioner is on the blink."

"You should call someone."

Gemma tamped down the anger that flared in her chest at her mother's patronizing tone. "I have. The parts haven't arrived." She inhaled for strength and gestured to the casserole. "What did you bring?"

"Lasagna."

"Oh, nice. Can you stay and eat with me?"

Phyllipa nodded, then frowned at Gemma's coat suspiciously. "It's ninety degrees outside. Why on earth are you wearing a coat, dear?"

Gemma forced a shrug. "The weatherman predicted rain."

Phyllipa squinted. "What kind of panty hose are you wearing?"

"Uh, they're part of my work uniform."

"Doing what?"

"I'll explain over dinner," Gemma said, turning toward the stairs. "Let me change first." She bounded up the stairs as fast as the high heels would allow, then closed her bedroom door and exhaled. Her mother's sense of timing hadn't improved.

With her skin still tingling from being caught in a compromising position, she crossed to the picture window and glanced down. Chev was in the yard, hosing off the newly tiled walkway and watering large trees still in tubs, waiting to be planted. His work shirt gaped open and she shivered, remembering the smooth firmness of his skin as he pulled her body close to his. She reached out and touched her finger against the warm pane of glass, imagining the heat they could generate.

At that moment he glanced up and saw her. He wet his lips and stared blatantly, expectantly. The urge to expose herself to him seized her. Moving automatically, she untied her belt and allowed the thin coat to fall to the floor.

Chev's hand slipped and water surged from the hose he held. Her chest rose and fell rapidly, the edge of the red corset biting into the tender flesh of her breasts. She slowly unlaced the front of the corset, then peeled it off, allowing her breasts to fall free. Chev turned to face her, legs spread wide, the water hose hanging loose at this side. His brown skin glistened in the waning daylight, his jeans riding low enough to reveal the white waistband of his briefs. Her gaze went to the bulge there, and intense feminine satisfaction welled within her. She reached up to cup her aching breasts, longing for release.

A knock at the bedroom door sounded, crashing into her trancelike state. She gasped, crossed her arms over her breasts, and turned away from the window. "Yes?"

"Gemma," her mother said through the door, "how about a nice salad?"

"Sounds good, Mom. Thanks. I'll be right down."

She pushed her hands into her hair and let out a sigh. What had she been thinking? Was she so out of control that she couldn't even restrain herself when her own mother was in the house?

She practiced deep breathing, counting to ten. Then, somewhat calmer, she dressed in jeans and T-shirt, ignoring the pings of the sensitive areas of her body. The window was like a magnetic field, pulling at her. She avoided it and went downstairs to face her mother, a stone of dread in her stomach.

Phyllipa had donned an apron and was rinsing romaine lettuce at the sink while the microwave hummed away, warming the lasagna. Gemma stopped at the doorway of the kitchen and pursed her mouth, because her mother's attention wasn't on the salad. Instead, she was craning to look out the window, presumably for a glimpse of the "strange man" that Gemma had been adhered to.

"Dad didn't want to come?" Gemma asked, snagging a tomato slice from a plate.

Her mother turned and wiped her hands on the apron. "He had something he needed to do."

A big, fat lie. "The lasagna smells great."

Her mother crossed her arms and assumed her parental stance. "So…are you going to tell me what's going on?"

Gemma felt herself being pulled along on the force of her mother's not-so-subtle guilt trip. "I don't know what you mean."

"Jason is barely out of the house and you've already taken up with someone else? Or maybe that was the reason he left in the first place?"

"No, that's not the reason," Gemma said through gritted teeth. "And I'm not going to explain my personal life to you, Mother."

Her mother screwed up her mouth, which was too bad, because otherwise Phyllipa was a very attractive woman. But Gemma had a hard time imagining her cold, uptight mother being warm and intimate. No wonder her parents seemed so distant from each other.

"Have you talked to Jason lately?"

"As a matter of fact, I called to ask him what to do with the things he left behind, and he didn't even have time to talk to me."

"He's a very busy man."

"I know, Mother. I lived with him for ten years."

Her mother began ripping the lettuce into chunks. "A marriage requires sacrifice, Gemma, especially when your husband has a demanding job." Phyllipa nodded to the stack of rolled-up newspapers by the door. "Since you haven't been keeping up with the news, you should know that Jason is in the middle of a very important drug case right now. I'm sure his stress level is through the roof. He needs all the support he can get."

A lump of emotion lodged in Gemma's throat. "Why are you making this out to be my fault? Whose side are you on?"

Phyllipa turned a compassionate eye on Gemma. "I'm on your side, dear. I want to see you safe and secure. Do you realize that Jason might be the next governor?"

Gemma bit down on the inside of her cheek. "This isn't what I'd planned either, Mom, but Jason has made it clear that he doesn't want to be married to me."

"Do you still love him?"

She hugged herself. "I...guess so. I miss him. I was

blindsided, so I'm still getting used to the idea of not being married to him."

Her mother came over and ran her hands up and down Gemma's arms. "If you love him, you have to fight for him, dear. He's probably going through a little midlife crisis. He'll be back when he realizes that he can't live without you."

Phyllipa smiled, her eyes bright with concern and sincerity, and Gemma felt her mother's love wash over her. She made the scenario that Gemma had initially fantasized about—of Jason coming back—seem possible. And preferable. But so much water had passed under the bridge…she was growing stronger and more independent every day, looking forward to finding her own way. "Mom, I'm not sure that I would welcome Jason back."

"That's your anger talking," her mother said quietly, squeezing Gemma's shoulders. "And you're entitled to it. But don't let it harden you to the possibility of patching things up with Jason. The best thing you can do right now is to let him cool his heels. He'll come to his senses."

Her mother had a way of making things sound so simple. *If only.* Gemma decided not to respond, to merely let her mother think what she wanted. In time Phyllipa would have to accept reality.

Her mother pulled her into a rocking hug, then withdrew and angled her head. "In the meantime, don't do something that might make it even harder for the two of you to reconcile."

The reference to Chev was unmistakable. Warmth flooded her face, but Gemma was saved from responding when the microwave chimed, effectively distracting her mother. She made it through the meal with small talk about the weather and asking about her mother's book club. When the subject of her job came up, she said she was working for a local museum.

"From the looks of the panty hose you were wearing, they must have a strange dress code," Phyllipa observed.

Gemma simply nodded and complimented the food. Fortunately, her mother didn't like driving in the dark, so she left soon after they were finished eating. Gemma stood on the porch and waved as her mother pulled away. When the car was gone, she stole a glance next door and saw that a few lights were on. Chev was still working, probably on the yards of wood molding that still needed to be repaired. The man obviously enjoyed working with his hands, but he was intelligent, too. And oh, so sexy in an earthy way that appealed to her baser instincts.

In fact, she wondered if her exhibitionism would have been so quickly revived if he hadn't been such a willing participant, located so conveniently next door, with a bird's-eye view into her bedroom. Probably not, she decided with a little bubble of resentment that she allowed to grow. He was, at least partially, responsible for her wicked behavior.

Feeling marginally absolved, Gemma turned and walked back inside, scooping up the unread newspapers. Her mother's comments about Jason had piqued her interest. She had to admit that she missed being in the middle of state politics.

Poring over the pages of the papers, her heart caught at the pictures of Jason at a press conference, or striding into the capitol building, looking as if the weight of the world was on his shoulders. A gag order had been issued regarding the drug case.

No matter what had happened between them, she still

respected him for rising to such an impressive office. He was, as her mother had indicated, probably headed for the governor's mansion. To think that she might have been the first lady of the state….

The phone rang, piercing into her thoughts, jangling her nerves. She glanced at the caller ID and noted it was coming from a private source. Afraid it was that pesky reporter Wilcox again, she almost didn't answer. After the fourth ring, however, she changed her mind.

"Hello?"

"Hi, Gemma."

Her pulse spiked. "Jason…hi."

"Did I catch you at a bad time?"

Gemma glanced around at the dark emptiness of the house and almost laughed. "No."

"I just called to see how you were doing."

She frowned at the slight slur in his voice. "Have you been drinking?"

"A little. It's been a rough week." His voice sounded raspy and unexpectedly sexy. She pictured him still at his desk, pulling at his tie, loosening the precise knot. His light brown hair would be ruffled from running his fingers through it. He would be drinking scotch, neat.

"I know. I was just reading in the paper about the drug ring you're prosecuting. You look tired in the pictures."

"I am tired," he conceded. "I'm sorry if I was short with you the other day when you called. It was nice of you to offer to send the things I left. Actually, I did remember a favorite golf towel that I misplaced."

"The black one? I found it in the garage."

"Uh, yeah, that's the one." He gave a little laugh. "It's my lucky towel. Did you throw it out yet?"

She leaned over and fished it from a cardboard box near her feet. "I suppose I could dig it out of the garbage."

"I would appreciate it." He exhaled heavily. "I'm so sorry, Gemma."

His admission took her by surprise, and she wondered with a pang of anguish if he was on the verge of confessing adultery. "Sorry for what?"

"I'm sorry for everything. I didn't mean to hurt you."

Her eyes grew moist as a host of emotions galloped through her chest—love, hate, regret, remorse, frustration. "Okay," she said finally, surprised at how steady her voice sounded.

"I could drive down in a few days to pick up that golf towel."

Her heart lifted unexpectedly. It was a flimsy excuse to come to see her. She fought to maintain a certain nonchalance. "That would be fine. I'll hang on to it for you."

"Great," he said, his voice warm and melancholy. "I'll come down as soon as I get a break from this case. Take care."

She hung up the phone slowly, not sure what to make of Jason's phone call. It seemed as if he was offering some kind of olive branch. Or was he reconsidering the abrupt end to their marriage? Maybe her mother had been right—that he'd gone through a bit of a midlife crisis, had wanted his freedom only to learn that it wasn't what he'd expected. Maybe he was starting to realize that she had been more than just a political prop, and that success is empty without someone to share it with.

The thought of getting back together with Jason made her mind spin in confusion. In the first few days after he'd left, she had fantasized that he would come back on his knees. But in the weeks that followed, her hurt had turned into anger. And when she'd received the final papers, she realized now that the anger had turned into resolve. Her thoughts were no longer dominated by Jason, her actions no longer dependent on him. Getting back together now seemed…retroactive. Things would have to be different, at least as far as she was concerned.

Then she chided herself for worrying about it. Jason might have been simply feeling guilty about the way he'd ended things, wanting to ensure she wouldn't have something bad to say about him in a subsequent election.

Still, she had to admit that knowing he might be having second thoughts was salve to her wounded pride. And the knowledge that she wasn't holding her breath after one tentative call from him buoyed her spirits. She felt better than she'd felt in weeks.

Maybe in *years.*

She was humming as she climbed to the second floor. She opened windows and turned on fans to alleviate the stuffiness. When she got to her bedroom window, the sight of the open round one across from hers warmed her midsection. And yet…

The talk with her mother and the subsequent conversation with Jason made her pause. Not because she was afraid she would sabotage a chance at getting back together with Jason, but because, she suddenly realized, she liked the feeling of being unattached.

She touched her mouth, remembering Chev's kiss. It would be easy to become attached to him, and she couldn't afford to do that now when she was just starting to get her legs underneath her again.

Gemma caught sight of the folded sheets of her fantasy

letter lying on her nightstand and was struck with the urge to keep reading. It was, after all, a harmless way to relive her fantasies. She moistened her lips and acknowledged a stirring deep in her sex at the mere prospect. Then she slid a glance toward the window and changed her mind. Reading more of the letter would likely only increase her eagerness to put on a show for Chev, and he'd already made it clear he wanted more than a performance…more than she was willing to give.

She glanced around the room, looking for a distraction. At the sight of her sketchbook, she brightened. She'd promised Chev she'd have the mural finished before his little family gathering. It was the perfect diversion from all the jumbled thoughts in her head.

From a hallway closet she retrieved a folded easel, a dusty tube that held a roll of primed canvas, and a suitcase containing her stash of paints, linseed oil, turpentine and assorted brushes and palette knives. When she lifted the lid, a wave of nostalgia flooded her senses. The smell of the pungent linseed oil, the sight of curled tubes of paint, the comforting feel of a round wooden brush in her hand. She carried everything to Jason's office and set up an impromptu studio, her excitement growing as the room took shape.

Gemma used a utility knife to cut the canvas to the size she'd jotted down in her notebook, then used thumbtacks and clips to fasten it to the easel. There was something so optimistic about a piece of clean white canvas—she could make it anything she wanted. She took a few moments to picture in her mind a replica of the simple gestural landscape that had once adorned the kitchen wall of the Spanish house. With a vine of charcoal, she sketched the picture onto the canvas. When she was satisfied that it was a close rendering of the sketch she'd shown Chev, she wiped her stained fingers on a towel and stood back with a smile.

She missed the therapeutic power of creating art. Creating something where once there had been nothing, something that had never before existed, could be a magical, insular experience. It had a way of crowding out everything else.

Then the screech of the peacock cut into the night air.

Gemma grimaced. Well, almost everything.

As the bird continued its grating call, she remembered what Chev had said about the creature, that biology would drive it to leave if it didn't find what it was looking for—a hen with which to mate. And she got the feeling that Chev was hinting that he, too, couldn't wait forever for what he wanted—*her*.

The difference, she reminded herself, was that unlike the peacock, Chev Martinez would be leaving no matter what. No-strings sex would be the perfect solution, but she knew she couldn't sleep with her seductive neighbor and not feel something…and she didn't want to go there. From now on, she would be on her best behavior, which meant staying away from her window, no matter how desperate she was.

Gemma swallowed hard.

And no matter how tempting *he* was.

13

"SO HOW'S THE HUNKY NEIGHBOR?" Sue asked.

"Fine," Gemma answered cautiously into her cell phone. Over the past couple of days she and Chev had fallen into the role of…cheerful neighbors. He helped to chase the bothersome peacock from her yard, she answered any questions he had about the house and worked on the mural in her free time.

And she scrupulously avoided her bedroom window.

Meanwhile, he had respected the distance she'd put between them since her mother's visit, with no questions. Although when they'd discussed the mosaic for the pool renovation last evening, she had felt his hungry gaze on her.

And she'd reveled in it.

"I think you should go for it," Sue said, as if she could read her mind. "He sounds like the perfect prospect for a rebound affair. I say the sooner, the better."

Gemma stretched forward to glance at the steel-gray clouds hanging low that did not bode well for a quick commute to the museum. "What, is there a clock ticking on my sexuality?"

"You said he's not going to be around for long."

"And?"

"And Dr. Alexander would tell you to follow your instincts."

"Dr. Alexander isn't around," Gemma said. If she were, Gemma would be tempted to tell her that the little experiment in class ten years ago had nearly been her undoing—then and now.

"Are those letters of yours giving you any ideas?" Sue asked in a suggestive voice.

"They're the words of a naive schoolgirl," Gemma said, as if she were trying to convince herself. "Let's just say they have no basis in reality."

Sue laughed. "But then reality can be such a drag."

"Have you talked to Jason?" Gemma asked to change the thorny subject.

"Not for a while," Sue said, her voice cagey. "Has he called again?"

"No."

"Good. I hope he doesn't."

"Sue, for heaven's sake, don't you think that Jason and I should at least be friends?"

"I just don't want you to fall under his spell again."

Gemma laughed. "You make it sound like I have no power to resist him."

"Jason makes his living persuading people, Gemma. And he's the only man you've ever slept with—that's powerful stuff."

"You're jumping to conclusions. Jason didn't say anything about wanting to get back together. And I didn't say anything about wanting him to."

"But you do."

Gemma sighed. "Okay, maybe a tiny part of me would like the satisfaction of hearing him say he made a mistake. Is that so wrong?"

"No," Sue admitted. "I just think you're on the verge of having your own life, and I don't want to see you get folded back into Jason's."

Gemma didn't respond, fighting unexpected pangs of doubt. Having her own life was being dressed like a call girl, on her way to a job that would mortify her parents— and Jason. And looking forward to it, God help her. Especially since she hadn't been getting her fix at home, exhibiting for Chev.

Rain splattered on the windshield. "It's starting to rain, so I'll call you later, okay?"

"Okay, bye."

Gemma hung up just as the gray sky unleashed on the city. She flipped on her headlights and wipers and slowed to accommodate the low visibility. She wondered how the weather would affect attendance today at the museum.

She parked in the museum employee lot, then ran through the rain that was now coming down in sheets. Poor Chev—the pool excavation would be stalled in this soup.

In the lobby, she shook her umbrella and smiled at Lillian, who had also just arrived.

"Join me for a cup of coffee?" Lillian asked.

Gemma nodded, shivering. By mutual agreement, they kept their coats on to cover their risqué outfits when they went into the break room and poured steaming cups of coffee. Gemma added creamer to hers, Lillian took hers black. They sat at a table in the corner.

"Nasty day," Lillian offered.

Gemma nodded and sipped the scalding coffee.

"You look a little down," the woman offered. The pink streak in her hair matched her youthful attitude. "Want to talk about it?"

Gemma shrugged. "It's nothing specific. Did you ever feel as if your life hadn't turned out the way it was supposed to?"

Lillian's extraordinary violet-colored eyes danced with good cheer. "I guess I didn't plan that far ahead. I tend to take happiness as it comes, and other than my brokerage account for retirement, I try not to outthink tomorrow." She smiled into her coffee, then took a generous sip.

"Easier said than done," Gemma said wistfully.

"Not really. I'm a tad older than you, so maybe that gives me more perspective. But the only times in my life I've ever been unhappy were the times I was living to make someone else happy—my parents, a boyfriend, my husband."

"You were married?"

"For five glorious years…and two horrible ones." Lillian gave a little laugh.

"I'm divorced, too," Gemma said, and realized it was the first time she'd said the words aloud without flinching.

"Life is too short to be with someone who doesn't make you happy."

Two male employees came in and looked their way while they filled their coffee cups, devouring the women's legs, Lillian's in sheer black stockings, ending in black stilettos, Gemma's bare and tanned, ending in red peep-toe platforms. Gemma felt a little rush of adrenaline, and noticed that Lillian sat taller, too. The men smiled and waved, then left, exchanging regretful glances.

Gemma ran her finger around the top of her coffee cup. "But what if what makes you happy…isn't good for you?"

"You mean like drugs or alcohol?"

"No…this is a different kind of addiction."

Lillian nodded thoughtfully. "Does it hurt anyone else?"

"No...the participants are...willing."

"Does it expose you to harm?"

"Not if I'm discreet."

The woman smiled brightly. "Then what's the harm?"

"The guilt," Gemma whispered. "And I'm afraid it will keep me from growing close to someone."

Lillian took another drink of her coffee. "Did your ex go along with it?"

Gemma wet her lips. It was strange—and liberating—to talk to another admitted exhibitionist. "No. He knew nothing about it."

"And were you close to him?"

"As it turns out, no."

"So depriving yourself didn't bring you the closeness you crave either, did it?"

Gemma shook her head, realizing the woman spoke from experience.

Lillian patted her hand and lowered her voice to a whisper. "So why deprive yourself? The right man will accept you and all your delicious inclinations." She glanced at her watch. "We're up in fifteen minutes, and I'd like to stop by the ladies' room. See you later?"

Gemma smiled and nodded, then sat at the table a little while longer looking for answers in the depths of her coffee. She wished she had Lillian's fearless outlook, could be so comfortable with her *inclinations.* She took a drink from her cup, remembering that for a few weeks during her senior year in college, she *had* been fearless.

But her fearlessness had also nearly ruined her life.

She turned her mind away from the disturbing murky memories, then emptied her cup. Still nursing more questions than answers, Gemma walked toward the cloakroom. The woman at the counter smirked when Gemma shrugged out of her coat, revealing her short red skirt and white bustier. Gemma ignored the woman's slight because her midsection was already tingling at the anticipation of leading the first tour of the day. When she walked up to the meeting place, she saw that the rain hadn't hurt today's reservations. If anything, the crowds were more swollen than usual.

The tours lasted anywhere from forty-five minutes to an hour, at the discretion of the guide, with a fifteen-minute break in between each tour. Gemma finished two tours before lunch, then ate with Lillian in the employee break room. It was becoming a habit, chatting away the hour. Lillian seemed to always know what to say, steering clear of talk about family and Gemma's ex, keeping the conversation light and breezy. The woman was well traveled and well read, with a wicked sense of humor.

Gemma laughed at something that Lillian said and realized with a start that she and Chev were the only people in her life who didn't know or weren't somehow connected to Jason.

Then bizarrely, she heard Jason's name on the television mounted high in a corner of the break room. She glanced up to see a clip showing Jason artfully dodging questions about the prosecution of the statewide drug ring that she'd read about in the papers. He sat behind a grand desk in what appeared to be his new office. His framed law degree hung on the wall behind him, and Gemma wondered idly what he had done with the photo of her that had once sat on his desk, wondered what the view was like from his office window. And was that a new suit? Her chest tightened unexpectedly at the proof that there was now a big chunk of his life that she'd been excluded from.

"He's handsome in a scholarly sort of way," Lillian offered, noting Gemma's sudden interest in the TV.

"Yes, he is," Gemma murmured. Her tongue watered to say the words that until recently she had been married to the handsome, powerful man. But she was mindful of the need for discretion in revealing her relationship to Jason to anyone she worked with. If word leaked out that she was giving tours for an X-rated exhibit, the press would have a field day…and her "delicious inclinations," as Lillian had called them, would be exposed.

"Funny," Lillian said, "but I pegged you for liking a different kind of man."

"What do you mean?"

Lillian shrugged her slender, toned shoulders. "I don't know, I just pictured you with someone a little more… free-spirited."

Gemma didn't respond, but the image of an exotic, brown-skinned man rose in her mind.

Lillian wadded up the paper wrapper from her sandwich and grinned. "Life is a smorgasbord. See you out there." She pushed to her feet and walked away.

Gemma finished eating lunch and took a few minutes to freshen up. Two more tours to go before calling it a day. Her step quickened as she neared the meeting place and slid her mask into place. Her body was already smoldering from the morning tours. Beneath the red skirt, she wore a white thong that bit into her skin with the insistence of a lover. Her clit was swollen and sensitive from the constant friction…just the way she liked it. She'd have to take it easy this afternoon or she might lose control and wind up giving the wide-eyed attendees a show they hadn't bargained for.

She extended a smile to the people already gathered for the first afternoon tour. "Welcome," she said warmly.

"We've been looking forward to this all week," a woman said, gesturing to a man next to her that Gemma assumed to be the woman's husband. "Our marriage counselor suggested that we come."

"That's nice," Gemma said. "It'll be fun."

"I'm having fun already," a guy standing nearby said, eyeing her bare legs. Everyone laughed, Gemma included, identifying the resident flirt of the group. There was always one guy who thought he could tease his way to getting Gemma's number at the end of the tour. What he didn't realize was that Gemma's "watch and learn" mantra extended to more than just the tour.

The area filled with more people, all slightly damp from the rain still falling outside. Warm, moist bodies, producing pungent odors, shifting from foot to foot in anticipation. Gemma silently counted heads, then squinted. The man in the back dressed in dark slacks and short-sleeve formfitting white shirt looked like...wait a minute—it couldn't be.

Chev?

He gave her a little nod of acknowledgment, then his gaze flicked over her costume. He must have abandoned his work site for the day due to the rain. A bolt of pure sexual electricity lit up her body at the realization that he would be watching her on the tour...and watching other people watch her. Pleasure coursed through her, but she was suddenly nervous, smoothing her hair behind her ear and fidgeting with her hands. Her thong suddenly seemed even more invasive.

After a deep breath to calm her nerves, she asked for the group's attention and announced they were about to begin. "A reminder that no pictures are allowed for this exhibit. Please keep your cameras stowed at all times."

As she scanned the faces in the crowd, she stopped abruptly. Lewis Wilcox—the reporter who had tried to thwart Jason's election and who had left her voice messages since the divorce. Alarm washed over her. Did he somehow know her identity? At the moment he was staring at her legs. She held her breath, but when his gaze reached her face, he gave the mask no more than a cursory glance. She relaxed a little, conceding it was just bad luck that he would be the reporter the TV station would send to check out the tour *and* that he'd wound up in her group. At least she had the mask to protect her identity. She was grateful she'd never talked to the man on the phone, so there was no way he'd recognize her voice.

Chev was frowning at her and mouthed *Are you okay?* She nodded and gave him a singular smile, grateful for his concern, even if he didn't know the source. She started the tour and, within a couple of minutes, became immersed in her lecture. She tried not to seek out Chev's face, but she couldn't help it. If the man cut a sexy figure in his faded work clothes, he was devastating in dress clothes. Not surprisingly, he was garnering a few looks of his own from women in the group, but he seemed unaware. He seemed, she realized happily, to have eyes only for her.

CHEV HADN'T BEEN SURE what to expect, wasn't even sure he'd be able to get in Gemma's group. In fact, he'd first landed in a group led by a petite, curvy woman with a pink streak in her black hair. When she'd noticed him craning, hoping for a glimpse of Gemma, the woman had quietly asked him if he was looking for another guide. When he'd nodded, she had covertly pointed him through another door where he found Gemma corralling a crowd of about twenty-five people.

The sight of her in the sexy red-and-white getup made his mouth water and his cock twitch. Her legs were long and bare and tanned. And that black mask of hers made him feel…proprietary. It was as if they shared a secret over the heads of the other people standing between her and him.

As she welcomed the group and gave them a brief overview of the exhibit, his chest warmed with admiration. She was engaging, her voice low and husky. A natural performer, and these people hadn't even seen her best show.

She led the group into the first area that housed nude photography that dated practically as far back as the time when photography was first invented. She moved like a cat, her limbs lithe and limber, her curves straining against the confines of the snug red skirt and white bustier. He stayed in the back of the crowd, felt the temperature of the group's collective libido rise as she explained the risks taken by the models and the photographers to capture the provocative images.

His own fire was stoked higher, not by the pictures of the white-thighed women in the photos who hid their faces from the camera, but by the heightened color in Gemma's cheeks as she caught his eye. Her mouth curved into the most sexy smile, setting off the beauty mark near the corner of her mouth.

"Blondie's hot, isn't she?" a man next to him whispered.

Anger sparked in Chev's belly watching the man salivate. Protective feelings crowded his chest. He wanted to pick Gemma up and carry her out of there, but he knew she enjoyed this part of the job…being watched.

And who was he to get between her and her fetish? Nobody, just a guy passing through. One of the many drooling guys who enjoyed looking at her, except he couldn't get enough, was starting to feel compulsively… *attached*.

As the tour progressed, she exchanged frequent glances with him, her body language becoming more animated. His body responded in kind until his erection throbbed against the fly of his dress slacks, his balls full and achy. From the photography exhibit, she led the group into a room of sexual devices. She donned a pair of white gloves and removed a couple of the primitive dildos from their containers. He saw the man who had made the comment about Gemma being hot stealthily lift a cell phone and snap a couple of photos. Chev nudged the man's arm, then shook his head meaningfully. The jerk looked sheepish and put away the phone.

A slow burn was consuming Chev by the time Gemma led the group into the room housing sex furniture. Perspiration trickled down his back, and his hands fairly shook from wanting to touch her. She lectured on the surprising number of beds, swings, benches and chairs built through the ages especially to aid in having sex or having sex in more interesting ways.

Behind the black mask, Gemma's eyes were bright and her hands languid as she touched the sometimes humorous-looking contraptions. But some of the more modern pieces of formed maple and leather upholstery were beautifully crafted and sent his mind spiraling in carnal directions, picturing Gemma draped over the contours, positioning her supple body perfectly to receive his.

Chev gave himself a mental shake and exhaled slowly. His body was like a furnace and every glance from Gemma in her red-and-white peep-show outfit added fuel to his fire. Worse, he suspected every man in the group was on the verge of incineration. He didn't like the idea of other men looking at Gemma, sporting hard-ons for her, but he could tolerate it if he knew he'd be in her bed tonight.

In truth, he'd settle for watching her undress and pleasure herself.

But at the end of the tour, despite the fact that he was burning up for her, Chev didn't seek her out. He sensed that the more he behaved like a stranger, the more intrigued she would be. It was a tactic he didn't like, but if it gave him a chance to get closer to Gemma in the long run, then it was worth pretending. So when she bade the group good-bye and caught his eye, he nodded curtly and beat a hasty exit out of the museum.

The rain was still slashing down, but Chev skipped an umbrella. He jogged through the downpour to his truck and climbed inside, drenched. Driving his fingers into his damp hair, he exhaled loudly. He'd hoped the wetness would cool his desire for Gemma, but it hadn't.

And it was time to face the fact that his longing for her had moved from something physical to something essential.

14

AT THE SIGHT of Chev's receding back, unexpected disappointment billowed in Gemma's chest, leaving her breathless with confusion. Her watch-me games had never before included this element of...*loss*. Part of the thrill had been the fact that it was a stranger watching her, a person she would probably never see again. Performing for Chev had seemed safe because he was moving on in a couple of weeks. She hadn't anticipated missing him after he was gone. If this achy sensation was any indication of how she would feel when he was out of her life, she might be in trouble.

Gemma put her hand to her throat, felt the heat there. Having his eyes on her during the tour had heightened her excitement to nearly unbearable levels. It was as if he were next to her, stroking her, whispering in her ear. For the first time, she'd wanted the crowd to disappear and leave her alone with one man, this man who could bring her body to the brink of orgasm simply by raking his dark brown eyes over her. If Chev could do such amazing things to her erogenous zones with only a glance, what kind of havoc could he wreak with his hands...his cock? A shiver raised gooseflesh on her scorching skin.

After letting management know she'd had a reporter in her group, she moved through the last tour of the day like an automaton. The rain had diminished but the soggy drive home seemed so interminable she thought she might break through her skin. She couldn't wait to get home, but was half-afraid of what might happen when she did.

Chev's truck sat near the curb, empty, but lights were on throughout the Spanish house. Puddles of muddy water sat in his construction-torn yard. Her yard looked almost as bad from the rain and the mess that the peacock had left her with. She leaned forward and looked up into the bird's favorite tree but didn't see the telltale swoop of tail hanging down. Perhaps the weather had driven him on to fairer skies.

She pulled the car into the garage and walked inside, her heartbeat thumping wildly. Still wearing her thin raincoat, she climbed the steps to the second floor, barely registering the stuffiness of the still air. The rain falling on the roof of the house lent an insular, cozy feel to her bedroom. She donned the black mask and walked directly to the picture window, wondering if Chev would show up at his to watch her. When she pushed aside the filmy curtain, she inhaled sharply.

He was there, waiting for her.

The light in the room behind him silhouetted his wide shoulders and broad chest. Still in his dress clothes, he stood with hands braced on either side of the rain-streaked pane, his gaze dark and hungry.

For her.

Gemma shrugged out of her coat, let it fall to the floor. She loved the fact that the rain had fogged the edges of the glass, had softened her frame. The white bustier had constricted her all day, pushing her breasts up and out. Now her increased breathing threatened to spill them over the top of the garment. Her nipples were showing, hard and extended. She pressed them against the window, gasping at the shock of the coolness on the sensitive tips. Her eyes closed involuntarily against the sensations spiraling through her body. She wished she could make the session last but knew she was too wound up to draw it out.

When her eyes fluttered open, though, Chev was gone.

Gemma pressed a hand against the frame in distress. Rejection and shame washed over her. She turned away, panicked by the emotions bombarding her. She couldn't need this man…she couldn't. Tears of frustration welled in her eyes.

Then the sound of the doorbell pealed into the house.

CHEV WAITED in front of Gemma's door, water streaming off his hair and fingertips. Enough was enough. Watching her would no longer satisfy his lust for her. If she didn't answer the door, he'd leave her alone. Because as much as she obviously loved being an exhibitionist, he couldn't take it anymore.

He held his breath and listened for noise inside the house, any indication that she was going to answer the door. Several seconds went by…then a minute…then two.

Chev pulled his hand down his face in frustration and turned to go. So be it.

And then the door scraped open.

He turned back to see Gemma standing there, still wearing the mask and holding the black raincoat in front of her. Her eyes were questioning but unwavering.

He reached her in two strides and gathered her in his arms, lowering a savage kiss on her mouth. She came alive, responding with the intensity he'd known she possessed, her movements frantic and a little desperate. He backed her into the house and kicked the door closed. Her raincoat slid to the floor. Chev deepened the kiss, exploring her sweet mouth, the prospect of experiencing all of her making his hands quake.

Gemma moved toward the staircase and pulled him with her. She half reclined, half pulled herself up the steps backward with him on top of her, crawling over her to keep up with her, snatching a kiss here, dropping a bite there. She smelled of an enticing mix of earthy perfume and rain.

"I'm getting you wet," he murmured, licking the moisture from her collarbone.

"Yes, you are," she whispered in a husky tone that sent another surge of lust ripping through his body. With both hands, he nudged the red skirt higher to reveal the minis-cule white thong underneath. The knowledge that she'd been wearing it all day while he watched her at the museum sent a jolt to his balls. Taking advantage of the leverage the stairs provided, he knelt between her knees and lowered his head to capture the thin fabric in his teeth. When she moaned and thrust her hips up, he buried his head between her thighs and tongued her heated folds through the thin barrier, inhaling her rich, womanly scent.

She drove her fingers into his hair, urging him on. It was all the encouragement he needed to roll the thong down her legs for full access to the nest of light brown hair that at this moment held the answer to every question pummeling his body. He clasped her bare thighs and opened her legs wider to him, then lowered his mouth to her glistening sex, kissing, licking and sucking her engorged clit. Her musky nectar filled his mouth, fueling his desire for her to unbearable heights.

From her frustrated noises, he sensed that she, too, was close to the edge. "Please, Chev…please."

He stabbed his tongue inside her and moaned against

her sensitive pink flesh to send vibrations to her pleasure centers. Concentrating on her enjoyment helped to keep his own arousal in check. She came with a great anguished cry of satisfaction, her clit pulsing against his tongue, her knees squeezing his shoulders. Masculine pride filled his chest that he could deliver her to a place where only physical joy mattered. He allowed her to recover for a few seconds, but he knew his own body well enough to know that he couldn't hold out much longer.

He picked her up and carried her the rest of the way up the stairs to her bedroom. When he released her, she slid down his body with her arms looped around his neck, a sleepy, sexy smile on her face beneath the mask. He kissed her beauty mark, then claimed her mouth. He reached under the skirt to cup her bare ass in both hands, feeling her wetness on his fingers.

She pulled his damp shirt over his head, then unfastened the waistband of his slacks and lowered the zipper. Chev stepped out of them, shucking his waterlogged shoes and socks in the process. His briefs clung to him, his desire for her unrepressed. He reached for her, wanting to rid her of her clothes, but Gemma pushed him toward the bed and urged him to sit. Then she walked out of arm's reach.

When she began to unlace the white bustier, Chev leaned back on his elbows to enjoy the show. With the skirt rucked up, hugging her thighs, her bare, tanned legs looked a mile long in those red high heels. His cock surged. Clear liquid oozed out of the head that protruded from the waistband of his briefs, pooling on his stomach. She slowly unlaced the bustier and allowed her breasts to fall free. He groaned to see the magnificent globes up close, his hands itched to touch the distended pink nipples.

She turned away from him and gave him a coy smile over her shoulder, then shimmied the skirt down to her ankles. Her tight ass made his mouth water, but when she bent over to step out of the garment, the view made the moisture on his tongue evaporate.

"Come to me," he commanded, his voice hoarse.

She turned and walked to the bed, her breasts bouncing, her thighs still shimmering with wetness.

"Take off the mask."

She shook her head. "I like it better this way."

Not in a position to argue, Chev pushed off his underwear, releasing his raging erection. She climbed on top of him and wrapped her fingers around his dick. The sensation made him buck. He clasped her hand. "I have to have you now. Let me get a condom before I explode."

Gemma stopped and for several agonizing heartbeats, Chev feared she would say that she didn't want to have sex. She seemed to be balancing on some sort of precipice and for an angry split second, he thought it was good that she could trust him. If she said no, he would find a less pleasurable way to achieve his release, but another man who had been tantalized by her watch-me games might not be so accommodating.

"I have a condom," she said finally, then leaned over to a nightstand and removed one from the drawer.

Her ex-husband's condoms, he realized in a haze. With her hands on him, rolling on the thin sheath, he frankly didn't care where it had come from.

Chev flipped her onto her back and settled his body over hers. He feasted on her breasts, sucking and biting on her nipples until they were hardened and scarlet.

"Yes," she murmured. "Oh, yes."

Chev had always prided himself on taking it slow with his lovers, but with Gemma, he felt feverish. And suddenly, he couldn't wait any longer. He kissed her mouth and her neck, then entered her silky channel in one deep thrust. Her body clenched around his like an exquisite spring—he set his jaw against the tornadic pull of her core.

Even as his body found a rhythm with hers, something akin to fear reared in his chest…it had never been like this before. This…*force* that seemed to be drawing the life fluid out of him. She lifted her hips to meet him stroke for stroke, her nails digging into his shoulders. Behind the mask her eyes were glazed with passion.

He tried to maintain control, but within a few seconds, he felt his body racing toward paradise. Her cries escalated and she climaxed again, contracting around the length of him in waves. Chev surrendered to the power of her and shot rope after rope of his essence, shuddering at the sheer intensity of being emptied so completely.

When their moans had subsided, he lowered his body gingerly, careful not to crush her, and rolled to the side. Gasping for breath, he lay staring at Gemma's still-masked profile, reeling from the emotions plowing through him. When had this happened? When had he fallen for her? And what could possibly come of it?

As if by mutual consent, they didn't speak. The rain falling on the roof was hypnotic, prolonging their fantasy state. Dusk was giving way to darkness quickly, casting shadows across the bedroom. The scent of their lovemaking filled the air and incredibly, Chev wanted her again. He reached for her hand, twined their fingers. "Gemma—"

"Shh," she whispered, putting a finger to his lips. Then she pushed herself up to straddle him. Her magnificent

15

GEMMA LOVED to make love in the morning. She stretched her arms tall and her legs long until her muscles sang, then she smiled and rolled over.

But at the sight of Chev Martinez slumbering on Jason's side of the bed—his black hair stark against the white pillowcase, his gold earring glinting against his skin, his tattoo of a leafless tree vivid on his muscled shoulder—she panicked. His being here seemed so…wrong. She sat and pulled up a sheet to cover her breasts, still tender from Chev's skillful hands and tongue.

Sometime during the night the rain had stopped. The morning sun slanted in the picture window, casting harsh light on the aftermath of their night of unbridled sex. The air was ripe with the aroma of body fluids, with at least three spent condoms in view. The sheets on the bed were tangled and warm, the bedspread and decorative pillows flung to the far corners of the room. The black mask dangled around her neck. Her costume from yesterday lay in one pile, his clothes in another. The sight of another man's dress shoes on the area rug made her heart race. What had she done?

"Hey."

She jumped, then looked over at Chev's lazy morning smile. His impressive erection tented the sheet. His long bronzed limbs were sprawled across the bed, taking up an inordinate amount of space, crowding her.

"Hey," she said, wondering how to delicately diffuse the situation…erase the previous night…go back to the way things had been—safe.

He reached forward, turned her hand over in his and ran his thumb over her palm, sending vibrations up her arm. "Since you don't have to work today and I'm not expecting my crew for a couple of hours, how do you feel about making love in the morning?"

An alarm sounded in her head. This was too much, too soon…it couldn't go any further. She pulled back, careful to keep herself covered. "Chev, we need to talk."

His expression clouded. "Uh-oh, I know that tone."

The ring of the phone cut through the air like a knife. Knowing it was rude, but grateful for the distraction, she dove for the receiver. In the back of her mind, despite the bad timing, she wondered perversely if it was Jason calling.

She was officially losing her mind.

"Hello?"

Sue's voice came over the line. "Hey, there. Did I catch you at a bad time?"

Gemma shot a glance at Chev, who was watching her closely, his dark eyes too perceptive. "No, you didn't catch me at a bad time. What's up?"

"I feel bad about some of the things I said yesterday morning," Sue said. "I shouldn't have encouraged you to have a fling with your neighbor. It's none of my business."

Chev swung his legs over the side of the bed and pushed to his feet. Gemma watched him under her lashes, conceding a thrill at the sight of his lean buttocks and broad, muscled back.

"Are you there?" Sue asked.

"Yes, I'm here," Gemma said, yanking her attention back to the phone call. "And that's okay, you don't have to apologize."

With his back to her, Chev picked up his pile of clothes and walked across the hall to the bathroom. The door closed with a dull thud.

"Do you have company?" Sue asked, her tone suspicious.

"What? No, of course not." But Gemma heard the false, tinny ring to her own voice.

"Oh, my God, you do have company! It's the neighbor, isn't it?"

In her confusion, Gemma waited too long to respond.

Sue whooped. "Yes! Was it fantastic?"

Gemma stood and reached for a robe, eager to be covered when Chev reemerged. "Um…can we talk about this later?"

"Only if you promise me the play-by-play."

"Goodbye, Sue."

She was tying the belt on her robe when Chev came out of the bathroom, fully dressed. She finger-combed her hair self-consciously, hating the awkwardness that reverberated between them, hating that she was the cause. She sensed that with one signal from her, he'd carry her back to bed. Her nipples hardened and he noticed, but she crossed her arms over them.

"Do you want to talk about last night?" he asked.

"Not really," she said, being honest. She inhaled deeply, then exhaled. "I told you I'm better at keeping things at a distance."

"Really? Then you faked it pretty convincingly."

Her traitorous body started humming in remembrance. "Chev, we both know this can't go anywhere."

His dark eyes bored into hers for several long seconds, then he nodded. "You're right. I guess that's my cue to leave."

But when he turned to go, she experienced that same horrible empty feeling she'd experienced when he'd left the museum. She realized with a sinking heart that while her mind knew what was best, her body knew what *felt* best.

"Would you like to see the mural before you go?" she asked, gesturing to the room she'd turned into a studio.

He pursed his mouth. "Sure."

She led him inside the room, feeling a little lift at the sight of the simple but colorful landscape that had emerged on the piece of canvas.

He looked at it thoughtfully for a few seconds, so silent that she began to feel nervous.

"If you don't like it," she said hurriedly, "don't feel compelled to hang it."

"I think it's wonderful," he said solemnly. "You're very talented, Gemma."

A flush warmed her cheeks. "I haven't painted anything in years. I enjoyed doing it. It should be dry enough to install soon."

"Okay. I'll let you decide when," he said, his gaze level.

She realized he was referring to more than the painting. Gemma swallowed and nodded, following him downstairs. But she needn't have. After a glance at Jason's things still cluttering the living room, he was out the front door and had closed it behind him before she reached the bottom step. She glanced guiltily through the front window, wondering if any of her neighbors had noticed the strange man leaving her house at the unseemly hour. After deeming that Petal Lagoon was deserted, she heaved a sigh of relief, feeling as if she'd dodged a bullet.

Déjà vu. Like years before…a close call.

But on the heels of relief came that nagging feeling of watching Chev walk away…and not liking it. Still, she couldn't have it both ways, and this was how things had to be. She couldn't undo last night, but it would be foolish to let her relationship with Chev become more complicated.

She climbed the stairs and stepped into the shower brimming with self-recrimination. Leaning her forehead against the cool tile, she groaned. She should've maintained distance between them, like she'd planned. Then she wouldn't be haunted by the memories of making love with the man all night long. Her body sang with latent longing. Unbidden, delicious chills ran over her shoulders and down her arms.

The chemistry between them was undeniable, unbelievable. For the first time, she understood what Dr. Alexander had been trying to tell her female students about the almost magical occurrence of having sex with a partner who was physically compatible in every respect.

Gemma leaned back to let the warm water fall over her breasts and find a natural trail down to the juncture of her thighs. At one point last night, she had felt as if she were having an out-of-body experience. Dr. Alexander would definitely approve.

She had to admit that sex with Chev had been more satisfying than performing for him. On the other hand, performing for him had stoked them both to the fever pitch that had catapulted them into bed. And kept them there for hours and hours…and hours.

And while it probably wasn't fair, it was impossible not to compare his lovemaking to Jason's. They were, after all, the only two men she'd ever slept with.

Where Jason had been tentative, Chev was fearless.

Where Jason had been reserved, Chev was expressive.

Where Jason had been missionary, Chev was acrobatic.

But you can't stay in bed twenty-four hours a day, her mind whispered. And what happens after the spontaneous fire burns itself out?

Loneliness…

Sobered, Gemma climbed from the shower and forced herself to matters at hand. The museum was closed today, so she didn't have to work. She spent the morning paying bills and balancing her checkbook, a task that took twice as long as it should have because her mind kept straying to the noise of the equipment and activity next door. Then she reasoned that since the weather had improved, she might as well clean up the mess the peacock had created in her yard before the neighborhood association left a threatening note in her mailbox.

The mailbox…changing her name was one more thing she'd been stalling on.

She wondered if some small part of her thought that if Jason did return, seeing the mailbox unchanged would be a sign that their marriage could be repaired.

Adding to her mental to-do list, she gathered her yard tools, hat and gloves.

It was a glorious day in the neighborhood. The rain had given summer a nudge, turning pale greens to deep emerald and dark greens to teal. The bird-of-paradise plants had bloomed riotously, with vivid orange petals and arrow-shaped blue-and-white "tongues." From the thickened grass, Gemma picked up a vibrant peacock feather and stroked the fringed edges, admiring the iridescent colors of green and teal and gold. She shaded her eyes and looked up into the trees that the peacock had favored, but the flamboyant pest was nowhere in sight. After creating upheaval in her life, it looked like he had finally moved on.

As she raked the yard and filled lawn trash bags with debris, she found herself stealing glances next door. More trucks and bodies than she'd ever seen before rambled over the property, apparently trying to make up for the day lost to rain. She saw Chev moving among the men in his work clothes, a red bandanna tied over his jet-black hair. Just watching him interact with the other men made her midsection pulse and her breathing accelerate. He looked in her direction once, but she couldn't tell if it was accidental or if he was seeking her out.

But why would he? She'd made it clear that she didn't want to sleep with him again. She should be relieved that he had indicated he would respect her wishes.

Wait for her to make the next move.

Her body felt heavy and stiff with tension, feeling at war with herself. Part of her ached to feel Chev's touch, part of her was convinced it would only lead to heartache. She should have insisted that they keep things at a distance. Now things were complicated. Now her heart was involved, and it made her feel exposed in a way that performing for him at the window never had.

She dragged the bags of lawn debris to the curb. Gemma removed her hat and used a glove to wipe away the perspiration on her hairline. She stared at her mailbox, wavering. *Jason and Gemma White.*

A shadow appeared overhead, then a loud yelp sounded. Gemma cried out and covered her head with her arms. The wide-winged peacock landed gracefully on the mailbox with a sound like a heavy blanket being shaken over a bed. The blue bird tucked in his wings and stared at her, his long train of tail feathers hanging to the ground, his head bobbing. The precise crown of feathers on its head gave the appearance of a Medieval war helmet topped with a colorful brush. Indeed, he didn't look particularly friendly at the moment. He thrust his regal head forward and unleashed a series of high-pitched cries.

Gemma stumbled backward and fell hard on her tailbone, then put up her arm to ward off the bird in case he decided she looked…mountable. "Go away!" she shouted, flailing to get to her feet.

A strong arm hauled her up. "Are you okay?" Chev asked, his face creased in concern.

"I'm fine," she said, feeling foolish. And feeling something else at the familiarity of his touch.

He waved his arms at the bird until it flew up in the trees.

"I was hoping I'd seen the last of him," she muttered.

"He's stubborn," Chev admitted. "It might take more to get rid of him than you planned."

His words resonated with double meaning, but if his words sounded menacing, the mischievous twinkle in his dark eyes took the sting out of them.

"Thank you for rescuing me," she said. "Again."

"You're welcome. I also came over to tell you that the thermostat for your HVAC unit arrived. I have my hands full right now, but I was thinking I could come over tomorrow and install it for you."

She knew that his simply being in her house again would be a dangerous temptation. Gemma moistened her dry lips. "I have to work. Could you come over when I get home?"

His regard swept over her, grazing every nerve ending. "I'll be watching." Then he turned and walked away.

16

GEMMA'S PHONE RANG as she slid behind the wheel of her car for the commute home from the museum. It was Sue—again. Since yesterday morning her friend had left two messages to call, but Gemma hadn't yet because she didn't want to be grilled about Chev.

Yet at the third insistent ring she conceded with a sigh that she was only putting off the inevitable.

"Hello?"

"Well, it's about freaking time. I was ready to come see you in person to make sure you were okay."

"I've been busy," Gemma hedged, starting her car.

"Good. With the neighbor?"

Damn…just the mention of Chev made her heart beat faster. "Sue, you're making way too much out of this."

"Humor me, okay? There's nothing this juicy going on in my life."

"He's coming over to fix my air conditioner tonight. I wouldn't call that juicy."

"That depends on which tool he pulls out of his belt."

Gemma couldn't help but laugh at her friend's silliness. "When did you get so bawdy?"

"I'm envious. You have a sexy job and a hot new boyfriend."

"He's not my boyfriend."

"So you don't deny that he's hot?"

"No comment."

Sue laughed. "You don't have to tell me. I can hear it. When you talk about this guy, your voice gets all low and husky. You never sounded that way when you talked about Jason."

Gemma swallowed. The last thing she needed to be told was that her lust for Chev was so obvious. If Sue could pick it up over a phone line, Chev would certainly be able to tell when he came over tonight. After all, the man was so observant. The perfect audience…

"Congratulations, Gemma. I think you've officially turned the page."

Her friend's words conjured up an image of the fantasies letter folded on the dresser in her bedroom, the one she still hadn't been able to finish reading. But she felt its presence, waiting for her.

"Thanks for the support. I'm getting ready to head home, so I'll call you later, okay?"

They said goodbye and Gemma pulled out of the museum parking lot while digesting her friend's words. After a day of tours, her body was primed for passion. She'd thought of little more than Chev all day, and the intensity with which he'd made love to her. It was a safe bet that if Chev was in her house this evening, proximity alone would set carnal things in motion.

By the time she arrived home, the bikini panties she wore underneath a pair of black short shorts were soaked. One crew was leaving Chev's property, and another one seemed to be packing up. He turned his head as she drove by and she felt his gaze on her skin like a full-body caress.

A shiver skittered over her shoulders as she pulled her Volvo into the garage.

She entered the house and had barely set her purse and black mask on the kitchen counter when the doorbell rang. She tightened the belt of the thin coat that covered the costume of shorts and sleeveless white tuxedo blouse and made her way to the entrance, her pulse going haywire. When she opened the door, she was taken back to the first time she saw Chev standing on her threshold. Was it possible that it had been little more than a week ago?

His clothes were dusty, but his big brown hands and muscular arms were clean. His expression was friendly but guarded, his eyes slightly hooded as he glanced at her legs, clad in fishnet stockings. The bandanna covering his head and the tiny gold earring in his ear made him look like a pirate bent on plundering. His sheer maleness nearly took her breath away.

"Hi," he said, holding a toolbox in one hand, lifting a small cardboard box in the other. "One thermostat."

Considering how stifling the air had suddenly become, it had apparently arrived just in time.

"Are you ready for me?" he prompted.

"Oh…yes," she managed to answer past a tight throat. She stepped aside to allow him entry, but she nearly tripped over a box of Jason's things that she still hadn't gotten around to moving to the garage. The sight of the golf towel that he had asked about gave her pause.

Chev cleared his throat and pointed to the stairs. "Why don't I go ahead and get started?"

She nodded. "Can I get you something to drink?"

"No, thanks. It shouldn't take too long to make the repair."

He was already walking up the stairs, his broad body

nearly spanning the entire width of the staircase. She followed him and squeezed past him in the hallway, then headed to her bedroom to change. Being so close to him conjured up visions of being even closer to him. "How's the house coming along?"

"Ahead of schedule," he said, concentrating on the HVAC unit exposed by the folding door. "The electric and plumbing is finished, and most of the woodwork is ready to stain."

He went to the breaker box and flipped switches to cut the power. Without the white hum of appliances, the house was hushed and echoey. Chev turned a flashlight on the work area and began to install the new thermostat. Beneath his gray T-shirt, the muscles in his shoulders bunched as he worked, giving her snatches of the tree tattoo that she had traced with her tongue between bouts of making love.

"Wh-what about the pool?" Gemma asked, struck by the awkward juxtaposition of the domesticity of the situation and the underlying sexual current sizzling in the thick, warm air.

"I'm still trying to settle on a design for the mosaic, but I'm close. I'd like to finish it before my family gets here in—what?" He squinted. "Three days. I thought my sister and cousin might like to break it in with a swim."

Warmth spread through her. He was obviously an adoring brother and cousin. "The mural is almost dry."

"Great." He removed a wrench from the toolbox and glanced over his shoulder. "You're still welcome to come to the party."

She smiled and nodded, but didn't commit. She barely knew him. Meeting his family was too…familiar. There was no point. All that existed between them was physical. And fleeting.

From the way Chev's jaw tightened, she had a feeling

he had read her mind. He looked as if he might say something, but changed his mind and turned back to the job.

"I'm going to change," Gemma murmured, and stepped into the bedroom. Although when she crossed the threshold, it was hard not to remember the way her bed had looked with Chev's big bronze body sprawled across its width. She closed her eyes against the erotic images and untied the belt on her coat.

"Can I watch?" he asked from directly behind her.

When she turned, he was standing in the doorway, one hand braced on either side. The hunger in his eyes ignited a fire in her midsection that threatened to consume her. She slowly unbuttoned her coat, then allowed it to fall and puddle around her feet.

A guttural noise sounded from his throat and his hands tightened around the door facing.

He wanted to touch her, but she appreciated his restraint. He knew how much pleasure she derived from him watching her. The anticipation was such a rush, Gemma felt lightheaded.

She unhooked the top button on her blouse to reveal a glimpse of cleavage and a lacy see-through bra. She was rewarded with his slow exhalation and the growing bulge behind the zipper of his jeans.

Then a foreign noise cut through the haze. Chev turned his head and straightened, a frown passing over his face. And before she could ask what was wrong, another man appeared in the doorway, his body language explosive, his eyes wide and bewildered.

Gemma's heart nearly stopped. *"Jason?"*

17

GEMMA'S MIND CHUGGED to process the surreal scene. Her ex-husband stood in the doorway of her bedroom in a dark, elegant suit, frowning back and forth between her and Chev. In his hand he gripped a bouquet of white lilies—her favorite, she registered vaguely.

"Gemma, what's going on?" Jason gestured to her outfit in dismay. "What are you wearing? And who the hell is this man?"

She opened her mouth, but no words seemed forthcoming.

Chev stepped forward. "Wait a minute, buddy. You're the one who just waltzed in as if this was your house."

Jason's head snapped back. "This *is* my house, *buddy.*" Then he looked at Gemma. "The doorbell isn't working."

"The electricity is off," she murmured. Not exactly the first words she thought she'd utter when she saw Jason again. She glanced down and realized her bra was showing, then hastily refastened the button. "This is Chev. He's... fixing the air conditioner."

The men sized each other up. They were about the same height. Chev had twice the bulk, and Jason, twice the attitude. Testosterone bounced around the confined space like rounds fired from a weapon. Gemma felt claustrophobic and sick, unsure of what was about to transpire.

"Are you almost finished here?" Jason asked Chev, nodding toward the open mechanical closet.

Chev's jaw hardened. "Yeah, I'm almost finished."

"Good," Jason said, eyeing the man suspiciously. Then he looked at Gemma. "I'm sure you'd like to change. I'll wait for you downstairs."

She exchanged an unreadable glance with Chev, then closed the bedroom door and hurriedly changed into jeans and a T-shirt. Her stomach was knotted with nerves, and her hands shook. The shock of seeing Jason again, seeing him toe to toe with Chev, left her breathless and confused. Why was Jason here? And how did she feel about him being here?

She breathed deeply to calm her racing pulse, but when she emerged, she still felt flustered. Chev was standing in front of the breaker box, flipping switches, his expression stony. Zone by zone, the electricity came back on, lights and appliances buzzed to life. Then he went to the wall thermostat and adjusted the temperature until the air conditioner clicked on. He reached up to hold his hand over a vent and grunted. "Cool air."

She wrapped her arms around her waist and made herself smile. "Thank you."

He leveled his dark gaze on her, then nodded curtly. "You're welcome. Now you don't have to worry about opening your windows."

Humiliation stained her cheeks. She swallowed past a tight throat but couldn't respond.

He leaned over and picked up the toolbox, the tattoo on his arm jumping. "I'll see you around."

She followed him downstairs where Jason stood like a sentinel watching Chev. Jason reached into his inside jacket pocket and withdrew his wallet. "What do I owe you?"

Mortification bled through her. "Jason—"

Chev glanced at the wad of cash her ex held. "It's already been taken care of." He looked back at Gemma and pursed his mouth, then opened the front door and walked out, leaving it open. When Gemma went to close it, she caught sight of his back receding, his shoulders taut. And she got the same empty feeling in her stomach that she'd felt before.

"Is that the neighbor guy your mother saw you with?"

Gemma closed the door and turned to face Jason. His pale blue eyes burned with...*jealousy?* The injustice of the situation sent anger galloping through her. "That's none of your business, Jason. And for the record, this is *my* house, remember? And why are you talking to my mother behind my back?"

"She called me. She was concerned about you."

"She doesn't need to be."

"Really? What's with the skimpy outfit you were wearing?"

Gemma frowned. "It's a costume. For a legitimate job."

He picked up the black mask from the counter next to where he'd laid the sheath of flowers. "What kind of a legitimate job requires a disguise?"

A flush climbed her neck. "It's only temporary."

"You got that right." He held up his cell phone. "Lewis Wilcox, the news reporter who dogged me during my entire campaign, sent a couple of photos to my phone this morning."

The tone of his voice alone was enough to cause her heartbeat to accelerate. When she glanced at the small screen, her worst fears were confirmed. It was her, leading a museum tour in the red skirt and white bustier, holding one of the primitive dildos. She was masked, of course, but the next photo was a close-up that clearly showed the beauty mark next to her mouth.

"I took a job as a tour guide at the museum."

"For an X-rated exhibit? What were you thinking?"

She moistened her lips, trying to keep the panic at bay. "I was thinking that I needed to take what I could get and work my way up. I was careful to use my maiden name on the application. I was told that the identity of all of the tour guides would be kept confidential for security reasons."

One side of his mouth slid back. "If Wilcox thought it was you, all he had to do was look for your car in the parking lot and run the plates."

Alarms sounded in her head. "Why would he send these photos to you?"

"Blackmail. He said he'd go public with the fact that you work the exhibit unless I gave him details of the drug case I'm prosecuting."

"I thought a gag order was in place."

"That's right."

Her eyes filled with sudden tears, realizing the precarious situation she had put him in. Full-blown panic flooded her limbs. "I'm sorry, Jason. I never meant for this to happen."

To her surprise, he put his arms around her and made soothing noises. "Don't cry. Everything's going to be okay."

She leaned into him and inhaled his familiar scent, recognized the familiar planes of his lean body. He lowered a kiss on her hair and tightened his grip.

"I'm the one who's sorry," he said, his voice breaking.

Gemma pulled back cautiously. "What do you mean?"

His expression was contrite and she was astonished to see tears in his eyes, as well. She had never seen Jason moved. "I made a mistake. I want us to try again."

Gemma saw stars. "What?"

He loosened his tie—one that she'd lovingly selected for his last campaign. "I'm an idiot. I had the world's greatest, most beautiful wife, and I messed it up."

Salve to her wounds, to be sure, but she was wary of his apology. "You said our marriage wasn't working for you anymore."

Jason shook his head and paced a few steps. "I mistook comfortable for monotony. I realize now that we were just going through a slump after the craziness of the election." He stopped pacing and pulled her into his arms. "I want you back, Gemma." He lowered his mouth to hers for the kind of kiss that she'd yearned for from her husband for as long as she could remember…a hot, intense meeting of tongues and teeth, with body language to match. He ran his hands down her back and pulled her hips against his, making the little grunting noises that she knew meant he was getting turned-on.

Gemma's mind reeled, but the seriousness of the situation kept her senses in check. She pulled back and walked away from him to lean against the breakfast bar and regain her composure. "Jason, I don't know what to think. This is just…so sudden." She crossed her arms over her chest. "I'm just now getting past the hurt. Starting over."

"With that guy?" Jason asked, jerking his head in the direction Chev had gone.

"Chev has been a gentleman. A good friend, who helped me when I needed it most." Helped her feel desirable again.

Jason pulled his hand down his face and suddenly looked tired. "It's my fault. I should've never moved to Tallahassee without you."

"But you did," she murmured, and the pain felt fresh,

slicing her heart open again, the same way it had when he'd first told her he wanted a divorce.

"Come with me now," he said, clasping her hands. "*We* can start over. Get married again, take a honeymoon. We'll tell everyone it was just a misunderstanding. Your parents will be so happy. And I'll make you happy, too, Gemma, if you'll just give me another chance."

Emotions assailed her from all directions—guilt, regret, remorse. Feeling under attack, she stiffened and pulled her hands from his. "I don't know, Jason. You blindsided me... again. I need time to think."

"Of course you do." He touched her cheek in a way that dredged up memories of good times together. "But the sooner you decide, the sooner we can get back to the way things were meant to be. I love you, Gemma, I realize that now. We can still have the wonderful life we planned." He nodded toward the cell phone that he'd set on the counter. "Dressing like a call girl, giving sex tours. That's not you, Gemma."

She swallowed hard.

"Let's try again," he said earnestly. "I can protect you from Wilcox if we get married again, if we're together."

Just the mention of the reporter's name made her stomach clench with dread. If he splashed her picture across the news, everyone would know—Jason's colleagues, the people with whom she used to raise money for charity, her parents. The shame, the scandal would humiliate her family and friends, and it would haunt Jason's political pursuits. What had she done?

Jason kissed her tenderly, and when she closed her eyes, she could almost forget that they had ever been apart.

"I'm going to be governor one day," he whispered fiercely, "and I want you by my side, Gemma. But it's up to you."

A panicky voice inside clamored for her to say yes on the spot. *Leave with him...before he changes his mind. Before you change your mind.*

The last thought shook her to her center. She gently broke free of his embrace and exhaled. "I'll think about everything you said."

He smiled the hopeful, boyish smile that reminded her of the way he had been when they'd first met, full of optimistic ambition that no one questioned, including her. She'd felt so lucky simply to be included in his plans. She walked with him to the door.

"I won't sleep until I hear from you," he said, with one hand on the doorknob.

She smiled, then her eye landed on the golf towel he'd asked about. She scooped it up and handed it to him. He took it, but glanced at it with an odd expression, as if it wasn't nearly as important as he used to think.

"If Wilcox tries to contact you, call me ASAP." He kissed her again and this time she tasted his desperation. He was worried...and it scared her.

She stood at the window and watched his car lights back down the driveway. When he pulled up next to the mailbox, the car paused. Was he checking to see if she'd removed his name? Then he pulled away from the curb and his taillights disappeared.

Gemma released a pent-up breath and massaged the sudden ache at her temples. With no appetite for dinner, she extinguished the lights and climbed the stairs, reveling in the cool air circulating once again. Her mind and body felt battered from sensory overload...the decision at her feet felt more weighty than she would've thought possible.

She considered calling Sue, but she already knew that her

friend would tell her to get on with her life—*without* Jason. Her friend's loyalty was touching but probably a tad biased.

Her mother, on the other hand, would tell her she'd be a fool not to go back with Jason and live a life of some celebrity and relative ease.

Regardless, she was glad she hadn't responded immediately, that she had held on to her pride by not jumping on his proposal to get back together, but also that she hadn't allowed her anger to cause her to reject him outright. She owed it to herself to consider his offer, if only out of respect for the years they'd been together. After all, she had invested a lot of time in Jason's success.

Gemma downed aspirin for the headache, then took a warm shower and poured herself a glass of chilled wine. Wrapped in a lightweight robe, she settled in an overstuffed chair in her bedroom and nursed this strange new sensation regarding her relationship with Jason—*power.* He had never been abusive, but there had never been any doubt who had been in the driver's seat in their marriage.

Because she had cared more about him than he'd cared about her. And the person in the relationship who cared less always had more power.

She could picture Dr. Alexander standing in front of the class saying those words, explaining the dynamics of any relationship, but especially between lovers.

The folded fantasies letter on the dresser called to her. Gemma retrieved it and, after another mouthful of wine, unfolded the flowered pages. She skimmed the slanted script, noticing that when she described her bouts of exhibitionism, her writing became less legible and more frenetic. She picked up reading where she'd left off, after the scene in the workout facility where she had performed for the young personal trainer while everyone else in the gym had been oblivious.

After leaving the gym, my urges were satisfied for a while. I went about my schedule as usual, and had decided that it was some kind of kinky phase I'd gone through. But two days ago I woke up with the familiar tingle of anticipation between my legs. In class, my mind wondered to scandalous places, like what the male instructors would think if I opened my legs to flash the color of my panties...or loosened the top button on my blouse and bent over to pick up a dropped pencil to give them a good view of my cleavage.

I met up with Sue for lunch and she told me about a guy she wanted me to meet, a friend of hers in law school who was in town for a few days. She said he was straitlaced, just my type, and I laughed to myself—she has no idea what my "type" is. I told her thanks, but no thanks. I had other plans.

While traveling around the city on the train system, I've noticed handbills for a "gentlemen's club" advertising amateur night. I'd decided that's where I was going last night.

Gemma inhaled a sharp breath and poured herself another glass of wine. The anxiety building in her chest was crushing, but she forced herself to read on. Her handwriting changed yet again, now nearly a scrawl, as if she hadn't wanted to document what had happened next.

The strip club was easy enough to find, but I confess I had reservations before going inside. I'd never been to a strip club before—I was a nervous wreck. I wore the brown wig and big sunglasses, and beneath a tailored trench coat, a bikini and high heels. I walked in behind two tall blond girls who seemed to know where they were going. When we were inside, one of them turned to me and asked if I was new. I held up the handbill advertising amateur night and they told me to follow them.

Once inside, some beefy guy asked if I was twenty-one and I said yes. But since he didn't ask for ID, I'm not sure he cared. I signed up as "Jewel" and was sent backstage for more instructions. There were a half-dozen other women, most of them young, who were listening to a woman named Breeze give advice on how to make an entrance, how to work the stage, and how to exit once our routine was finished. We could take off as much or as little clothing as we wanted to. We were allowed to keep our tips, and were promised that a bouncer would always be between us and customers who might try to manhandle us.

When the music started blaring, everyone seemed nervous—except me. I was breathless with anticipation as I watched other women go out and dance. Some of them were bad, but a couple of them were trained dancers and got the crowd going. I was last and when I stepped out on that stage still wearing wig, sunglasses and coat, something happened to me—it was like I was a different person.

It was a full house and the air was charged with sex. I've never been much of a dancer, but the music seized me and, running on adrenaline alone, I strutted up and down the stage, losing the coat to *reveal my teeny bikini. I had told myself I wouldn't get completely bare, but the excitement of the crowd, the excitement of being watched, buoyed me and instinctively, I unhooked the bikini top and the crowd went wild. I've never been so turned-on and next thing I knew, I was wearing only the stilettos, wig and sunglasses. I hadn't thought to wear a garter to hold tips, and frankly, I didn't care about the money that was tossed at my feet. I was in heaven with the eyes of everyone in the room on me.*

I was making my last trip back up the stage when the sirens sounded and the club lights came on. A man with a bullhorn announced this was a police raid and told everyone to freeze.

Instead, everyone ran. My life flashed before me: arrested, expelled from college, disowned by my parents. I somehow found my coat and was swept along with the crowd. It was pandemonium. I was terrified I would fall and be trampled. Breeze, who had been instructing the amateurs, grabbed my arm and pushed me out a fire exit door. When the police stopped us outside, she whispered for me to run, and I did…as if my life depended on it.

I managed to escape and ran until the crowd thinned. By that time I had twisted an ankle and was hopelessly lost. I threw up on the side of a deserted street. I was close to full-out panic when I realized my wallet was in my coat pocket. I hailed a cab, but it was after midnight when I got back to the dorm, carrying my shoes, still naked under the coat and wildly disheveled. I had tossed the wig and the sunglasses, but I still garnered some strange looks from

*my roommates. Sue, in particular, gave me the third
degree, but I begged a headache and went to bed.*

*I didn't sleep a wink. I kept thinking about how
disastrously the night could have ended. For me, acting
out my fantasy nearly led to my ruin.*

*And the worst part of it all? It's been only two
days and I want to do it again.*

Gemma pushed to her feet and paced, feeling flushed.
The bad memories from that night came back to her in
snatches of pure emotion—the shock of the raid, the horror
of trying to outrun the police, the fear that had lingered for
days that they would somehow discover she had been at
the club and come to arrest her. As it turned out, the club
had been a front for a drug operation. She had simply been
in the wrong place at the wrong time.

But at the time, it had seemed like retribution…karma
for doing something so wicked. The incident had, so to
speak, scared her straight. She'd told Sue she wanted to
meet her straitlaced friend and had latched on to Jason like
a lifeline. He had saved her from herself.

Gemma stared at the letter in her hand with disdain. Its
timely appearance had reawakened dormant impulses, had
sent her to the window to undress for Chev, had pushed her
into taking a sordid job at the museum. Once again, she was
on the verge of being revealed…and once again Jason was
in a position to save her. These subversive impulses of hers
could lead nowhere—nowhere good, that is.

She glanced at the picture window but forced herself not
to go there—literally and figuratively.

Gemma found a book of matches and lit one. With a
shaking hand, she held up the fantasies letter and lit one

corner. The pages began to char and curl, destroying the words and, she hoped, the urges they described. She dropped the letter into a metal trash can and drained her glass of wine while watching the flowered sheets of stationery disintegrate into a little pile of white ashes.

She had gotten another reprieve. She and Jason could marry again, quietly, maybe in Belize or Hawaii, and start a new phase of their life. She would slip back into her role as Jason's assistant, head hostess and all-around helpmate. He would appreciate her this time. They would be partners. He would be governor someday, then probably head for Congress or the U.S. Attorney's office. They would once again be the golden couple.

And she could put this naughty little exhibitionist phase behind her. Again.

18

GEMMA LOVED to make love in the morning. She rolled over and palmed the area of the mattress that, with a single phone call, would once again be occupied by Jason. He wasn't a morning person when it came to sex, but in the scheme of things, it was a very small price to pay. Marriage was more than great, earth-shattering, mind-bending sex.

The hum of the air conditioner filled the air. And even through the closed windows, she could hear the construction noises from next door.

Since Jason's visit yesterday, she had forced herself not to think of Chev, told herself that he couldn't figure into her decision to go back to Jason. He would, after all, be leaving soon. Their time together had been simply a pleasurable diversion, nothing more.

She reached for the phone to call Jean at the employment agency, planning to tell her that she was quitting her job with the museum. But at the last second, she instead dialed Lillian's cell phone number.

"Hello?" The woman's voice trilled over the line, low and honeyed.

"Lillian, it's Gemma."

"Hi, doll. What's up?"

"I…" Why did the prospect of telling Lillian that she

was quitting her job make her feel as if she was denying something they both knew to be true? "I'm not feeling well today."

"Oh, that's too bad. I can cover for you if you like."

She exhaled in relief. "I would appreciate it."

"No problem. I hope whatever's wrong will run its course soon."

The woman was nothing if not perceptive. "I think it will," Gemma murmured. "Thanks again for covering for me."

She hung up the phone, feeling torn. Why was she stalling on what seemed to be an obvious answer to her dilemma? Was she postponing her decision to prolong Jason's agony? Her attention traveled to the picture window. Or was she simply giving herself time to tie up loose ends?

"Chev?"

He turned his head to see his foreman's face creased in frustration. "Sorry, what?"

"Man, where is your head today?" Then the man looked past him to Gemma's house, and he scoffed. "Dude, you're worse than that lovesick peacock strutting around in her yard."

Chev straightened. "I don't know what you're talking about."

"Yeah, right." He clapped Chev on the shoulder. "We're ready to unveil the pool."

Reluctantly, Chev dragged his gaze away from Gemma's house. The peacock was back, parading around her yard, its tail unfurled, calling like some kind of horny lawn ornament.

He knew how the bird felt. He kept hoping Gemma would

emerge so he could rescue her from the nuisance again. A pathetic ruse, like thinking he could rescue her from her ex-husband last night. It was obvious she hadn't wanted to be rescued. She was still hung up on the guy. And why not? He was successful and powerful, not a jack-of-all-trades carpenter who moved around like a Gypsy.

But the man had also broken her heart. He couldn't love her if he had put her through that kind of torment.

"Whoops, here she comes," the foreman said. "The pool can wait until later."

Chev turned to see Gemma walking down her front steps wearing jeans and a sunny T-shirt, carrying what appeared to be a rolled-up canvas. To his dismay, just the sight of her made his big, stupid heart swell.

He had it bad for this woman.

He moved toward her at the same time as the peacock, who thrust its head forward and unleashed a torrent of calls. At her expression of half irritation, half fear, a pang of remorse struck his chest. She didn't need the extra aggravation of him or the bird in her life.

She hurried toward him, and the bird followed her as fast as its cumbersome tail would allow. He couldn't help laughing, though, and happily positioned himself between her and the peacock, stomping his foot to send it scrambling back to her yard, yelping.

"Hi," he said, smothering a smile.

"Hi," she said, her color high, her voice exasperated. "I'll be so glad to be rid of that bird!"

He arched an eyebrow. "Oh? Are you hoping it will leave, or are you planning to leave first?"

She averted her eyes and cleared her throat. "I'm sorry about last night. I…wasn't expecting Jason to drop by." She fidgeted. "He's a powerful man...he's accustomed to getting his way."

"I know who he is," Chev said. "I watch the news."

A flush climbed her face. "I didn't mean to imply otherwise."

"Does he want to get back together?" he blurted. As soon as the words left his mouth, though, he raised his hands. "I'm sorry, that's none of my business." But he could tell from her body language that he had guessed correctly.

She held up the canvas with a smile. "The mural is dry."

"Great. I have the frame ready, but I could use a hand installing it, if you have a few minutes." A thinly veiled excuse to keep her within arm's length.

"Glad to help," she said cheerfully, but her nervousness was apparent in the stiffness of her shoulders, her quick hand movements.

He wanted to say something to put her at ease, but it felt hypocritical when his unsolicited cock was swelling in his pants.

He led her into the house, which reeked of fresh paint and sawdust, and echoed with the sound of hammers in distant rooms finding their mark.

"Everything is coming together so beautifully," she said, running a shapely hand along the woodwork of the new chair rail that ran throughout the house.

He remembered exactly what it had felt like to have her hand running along the indentation of his spine. "Thank you. Your opinion means a lot to me. You've been so helpful, Gemma."

She smiled. "Speaking of helpful, the air conditioner is working perfectly."

"Good. So you slept well last night?"

She hesitated. "Reasonably well."

He held her gaze for a few seconds, trying to telegraph his hopeless feelings for her. Finally he smiled in concession. "I can't wait to see the mural on the wall."

Once in the kitchen, he held the end of the stiff canvas and allowed her to carefully unroll it, revealing the colorful, gestural landscape. Together they positioned it on the wall where the deteriorated canvas had been removed. Once the painting was centered, he tacked the corners with penny nails, then stood back to admire it. "It's perfect," he said. "It'll be a nice selling point, and I'm sure the new owners will enjoy it every day."

"I'm glad you like it," Gemma said, clearly pleased.

From the long farmhouse table, he selected the four pieces of mitered seasoned oak he'd carefully measured and cut. Using a drill, he put tiny pilot holes in the frame, then screwed them in place around the canvas. The effect was an old-fashioned built-in mural that might have been in the house for generations.

"Nice," he said, giving her a grateful smile.

"I guess this means we're…even," she said.

Chev knew a brush-off when he heard it. "I guess that means you won't be coming to the party tomorrow night."

"I don't think so. I might have to work late anyway."

He didn't believe her excuse, but he nodded.

"By the way, when you were at the museum the other day, did you happen to see anyone taking pictures?"

Chev frowned. "As a matter of fact, there was a guy with a camera phone. I let him know I saw him and he put it away."

"Not soon enough," she murmured.

"Is something wrong?"

"His name is Lewis Wilcox and he's a reporter. He

knows who I am—or rather, that I used to be married to the state attorney general. He sent the photos to Jason and is threatening to reveal everything."

Chev shrugged. "So?"

"So…it will be bad for Jason that I'm doing something so…controversial."

"But it's not illegal, and besides, you're good at it. And I know you enjoy it."

She gave him a tight smile. "Too much for my own good."

"Ah. Your ex doesn't know that you're…"

"An exhibitionist?" she said bluntly. "No. And I wasn't one when he and I were together."

"So this is something recent?" he probed, his balls throbbing just talking about it.

"No." She looked up, down, all around. "My first experiences were in college."

"And it started up again after your divorce?"

She nodded. "When you moved in."

He stepped closer and picked up her hand. "Look, Gemma, I'm no expert. But it doesn't take a psychiatrist to see that you're using this fetish to keep from getting close to someone."

"Maybe," she admitted.

"All I'm saying," he said gently, stroking his thumb over her palm. "Is that the two don't have to be mutually exclusive."

Her chest rose and fell as her breathing became more labored. The hardened points of her nipples showed through her T-shirt. Her lips parted and her eyes dilated. She wanted him, he could feel it. She was thinking about the night they'd spent together burning up the sheets, barely speaking because they hadn't needed words to communicate. They were communicating now, he realized as the air became thick with need.

"Gemma—"

She abruptly pulled her hand from his. "I have to go."

Chev didn't try to stop her. He had no right to.

SHAKEN, Gemma practically ran back to her house, dodging the peacock, which seemed determined to block her path. "Get out of the way!" she shouted, shooing the bird, thinking if it hadn't been for the pesky creature, she and Chev might not have interacted so much, and she wouldn't be...

Confused.

She closed the front door and leaned against it. It was the man's bottomless dark eyes, damn it. The way he looked at her...as if she were the only thing in the world that mattered. It was, she realized, why they seemed to have such a deep sexual chemistry. They connected through meaningful and purposeful eye contact.

It occurred to her suddenly that she and Jason had moved through their entire marriage making as little eye contact as possible. Was it because they each didn't like what they saw? Didn't feel the connection, so they'd found it easier and better to just stop looking?

Her cheeks were wet when she walked to the phone. She dialed Jason's number and he answered on the second ring, his voice pleased. "Gemma? I saw your name on the display."

"Yes, it's me."

"How are you?"

"Fine. Is this a bad time?"

"No worse than usual." He gave a tight little laugh. "Have you given some thought to what I proposed?"

To what I proposed. As if it were a business deal to be settled. As she listened to papers rattling in the background amidst keys clicking on a keyboard, her heart sank. He couldn't set aside work long enough even to talk about rebuilding their marriage. Was he so sure that she'd come running back to him that he'd already crossed it off his to-do list? Tears clogged her throat, but at least it confirmed her instincts.

And her decision.

"Gem, are you there? I don't mean to rush you, but I have to be somewhere in fifteen minutes."

"Of course," she said. "This won't take long. I've thought about what you said, Jason, and I've decided that I prefer to leave things the way they are."

Silence resonated over the line as the paper rattling and key clicking stopped. "I'm sorry—what did you say?"

She inhaled. "I don't want us to get back together."

Disbelieving noises sounded in her ear. "But…you're making a mistake. If we don't get back together, Gemma, I can't control Wilcox. You won't have the protection of my name or my office."

She pressed her lips together, biting down. It was so like Jason to try to exert pressure to get his way. "I hope he doesn't use those pictures to embarrass you or your office, Jason, but if he goes public with them, I'll be fine. I happen to like my job and frankly, I'm good at it." And she was no longer going to be ashamed of her "inclinations," as Lillian had so aptly put it.

"Gemma, why are you doing this?"

"Because I love you, Jason, but not enough."

"Not enough to what?" he asked, incredulous.

Gemma closed her eyes at his inability to grasp the

emotional gravity of the situation. "Exactly," she murmured, then hung up the phone.

She took a few moments to breathe deeply and to mourn the time lost. They both deserved better. She pushed to her feet and, eager to rid herself of all the artifacts of her marriage, carried the boxes and baskets of Jason's things to her trash bin in the garage. The divorce papers went in the file cabinet. Then she tackled the photos.

While she sorted through pictures of their life together, making a stack for herself and one to box and send to her mother, she slipped their wedding DVD in the player and let it run in the background. She'd watched it countless times during the divorce proceedings, but this time it was different. This time, she was dry-eyed and philosophical, wishing she could talk to the young bride in the film and tell her to run and find someone who knew everything about her—including her fetishes—and still wanted to be with her.

She smiled at the picture in her hand, one of her and Sue at a charity golf scramble from a few years back, their arms around each other's shoulders. But it was something in the background that caught her eye—Sue's golf towel… black with a gold letter monogram. Exactly like the one that Jason had seemed to prize, a gift from someone…

An awful seed of dread took root in Gemma's stomach. She picked up the remote control and went back to the beginning of the DVD, this time watching the interaction between Sue, her maid of honor, and Jason.

They'd stared at each other when Sue walked down the aisle, escorted by Jason's best man. After Sue took her place at the altar, there was an exchanged glance…then another…and another, each more lingering than the last. Even while Gemma walked down the aisle. Sue was nervous, fidgeting. Jason looked…uncertain. When he wasn't looking at her or Sue, he was looking straight up, as if he were struggling with a decision. And when the minister asked if anyone knew of any reason she and Jason shouldn't marry, Sue had opened her mouth…then closed it. Then *there*.

Gemma froze the tape. Jason had pivoted his head and looked at Sue, a pleading expression in his eyes. An expression of *love*.

She covered her mouth with her hand. Jason and Sue… how had she missed it? Snatches of conversation came back to her.

I never dreamed the two of you would get married… I'm just really happy that you're moving on…I don't want to see you get folded back into Jason's life.

Sue had scoffed at the idea of her getting back together with Jason…because she wanted him for herself? How convenient that she was in Tallahassee and so was Jason. And that he had left Gemma in Tampa.

With the frame of Jason looking at Sue over her head frozen in the background, Gemma picked up the phone and dialed Sue's number, her fingers shaking.

"Hi, Gemma," Sue sang cheerfully. "What's up with you?"

She gripped the phone, bile backing up in her throat. "How long?" Her voice quaked.

Sue gave a little laugh. "How long what?"

"How long have you and Jason been fooling around behind my back?" At the silence on the other end, tears filled Gemma's eyes. "Oh, God, it's true."

"Gemma, let me explain—"

Gemma disconnected the call and unplugged the phone, then hugged herself, every part of her aching. Her marriage had been a lie…Jason had never loved her. Her friendship with Sue, another lie. Their late-night gabfests in college, sharing hopes and dreams, long-distance phone calls when they'd landed in different cities after she'd married Jason, making it a point to never miss a birthday or anniversary of some special occasion. To think that she had relied on Sue's advice to get through the divorce. And to top it all off, she had slept with Chev at Sue's repeated encouragement to "go for it."

A few minutes ago, she had felt like an independent woman reclaiming her life, only to discover that she had been manipulated every step of the way. She had to be the world's biggest fool.

She put her head down on her knees. And the loneliest.

Outside the peacock emitted its high-pitched call. She was struck again by how similar it was to a person screeching, *Help! Help!*

Help was right. She longed to go to Chev, to escape in his arms tonight, but she didn't dare invest any more in a man who would be leaving in a few days. She couldn't afford to lose any more of herself.

19

GEMMA EXPECTED it to be a sleepless night, and she was right. Knowing that Jason and Sue were involved was like getting divorced all over again. The peacock, as if sensing her mood, wailed plaintively most of the night, keeping her company. She cried until she was sick for the wasted years with Jason, then lay awake dry-eyed as the sun came up and light crept across the room. The peacock had grown either tired or philosophical, since its cries also quieted at daybreak.

She didn't feel like going to the museum and she knew she was wearing her distress on her face, but she needed something to occupy her time. And frankly, she was once again in the situation of needing the money. So she showered, gulped down a cup of coffee and carefully applied makeup to hide the plum-colored circles under her eyes. Then she dressed in a fitted short black sheath and black pumps— demure compared to her other costumes.

As she made up her bed, she listened to the work site next door come alive with vehicles arriving, supplies being moved, and equipment starting. She would miss it, she decided, the comforting noises of the bustling activity. And she would miss Chev.

The doorbell rang and her spirits lifted instantly at the prospect of seeing him. She hurried down the stairs and swung open the door, but at the sight of Sue standing on the threshold, she balked. "What are you doing here?"

Sue had been crying, too, her dark eyes red rimmed. "Please…just hear me out."

Gemma didn't say anything, but stepped aside to allow her entry. Sue was taller, curvier, with flaming red hair that was always cut in the latest style. She swept by Gemma, then turned with a pained look on her face after the door was closed. "Can we sit down?"

Gemma nodded and waited for Sue to sit, then lowered herself in the opposite chair.

Sue's chest rose with a deep breath. "Gemma, I know you're hurting, and I'm sorry. I have a lot of things to apologize for, but I'm *not* having an affair with Jason."

Gemma crossed her arms. "There was a golf towel that was special to Jason, a gift from someone. I saw a picture where you have one that's identical. And I watched our wedding DVD—the way the two of you were looking at each other." She stopped, her voice choked.

Sue nodded slowly. "Jason was in love with me back then, but I never felt the same way about him. The golf towel was a gift from him, something he had made for us. When I introduced the two of you, I was hoping his feelings for me would go away. And I think they did…for a while. But I had my reservations about the two of you getting married."

Gemma swallowed past the lump in her throat. "But why didn't you tell me?"

"Tell you that you shouldn't marry Jason because he was in love with me?" Sue gave a dry laugh. "How would that have gone over? The way you fell for him, so fast, it was like you just *needed* him so much."

She had, Gemma conceded miserably. After the terrifying episode at the strip club, she had latched on to Jason for his strength—his feelings for her had been secondary. She had convinced herself that she cared enough for both of them.

"I just couldn't do that to you," Sue said with a teary smile. "So I moved to Tallahassee and hoped that Jason would realize what a catch you were."

"But he never stopped loving you."

Sue leaned forward. "I know he cares deeply about you, Gemma. He's told me so many times."

"But at the prospect of moving to Tallahassee, where he knew he'd be crossing paths with you, he couldn't take it anymore and asked me for a divorce."

Sue hesitated, then nodded. "I told him it was pointless, Gemma, but he did it anyway. He hated to hurt you, and didn't tell you why because he knew it would only hurt you more."

Gemma nodded. The divorce had devastated her, but knowing that he was in love with her best friend would have broken her. "You must have made it clear that you weren't going to marry him after all. Because he came back two nights ago, asking me to forgive him and to give our marriage another try."

Sue's mouth tightened. "I thought he might. What did you say?"

"I considered it," Gemma admitted. "But in the end, I couldn't do it."

A relieved smile lifted the corners of Sue's mouth. She leaned forward and grasped Gemma's hands. "I'm so glad. Jason is a great guy, but you deserve someone who adores you."

"That's why you kept encouraging me to have a fling, to get on with my life," Gemma murmured.

"It helped, didn't it?"

She laughed. "Yes. It did."

Sue squeezed Gemma's hands. "And how do you feel about this guy Chev?"

Gemma sighed and glanced in the direction of the Spanish house. From this angle she could see a portion of the pool, covered with a large blue tarp. "He's…fantastic. Sexy, intelligent, warm…sexy." They both laughed. "I think it could be special…but he's leaving in a couple of weeks, as soon as the house is renovated and auctioned off."

"Maybe he would consider staying."

Gemma shook her head. "The auction date is already set. And I don't think I'm ready to make that kind of commitment anyway. I jumped into a relationship with Jason. I don't want to do that again."

"Smart," Sue said, standing. "But you're older, and wiser. You know your own mind—and body—much better. Trust your instincts. You'll know if it's worth the risk."

"How about you?" Gemma asked. "When are you going to get someone special in your life?"

"Still looking," Sue quipped. "And always hopeful. If I could go back, I'd take that Sexual Psyche class with you in college. Maybe it would've helped me figure out a few things about myself."

"It helped me," Gemma admitted, then smiled a secret smile.

They embraced and Sue walked to her car after extracting promises to call. While Gemma stood at the top of the steps, waving, the peacock waddled up to the bottom of the steps and unfurled his tail in a spectacular iridescent fan.

The morning sun reflected a thousand brilliant colors in his magnificent plumage, shimmering against the dew-laden grass. The sight of him took her breath away, and in that moment, Gemma felt blessed.

Sue rolled down the window, her expression wondrous. "Looks like you have a pet."

Gemma laughed. "Since I can't seem to get rid of him, I might have to keep him."

Sue waved and drove away. Gemma looked down at the blue bird, who angled his head at her. "Looks like it's just me and you."

Her gaze wandered to the site next door, but she didn't see Chev among the workers. He would be busy today, putting finishing touches inside and out to get ready for his family's visit that evening.

There was that funny feeling in her stomach again…the "missing him" sensation. If only…

She glanced at her watch and gasped when she realized she was going to be late for work. She grabbed her coat and purse and backed out of the garage without incident— the peacock had found something to eat at the base of one of her trees.

On the way to the museum, she realized that she was actually humming, that she felt better than she would've imagined possible a few weeks ago. When she arrived at the museum, she looked for Lillian to thank her for covering for her the previous day. She found her in the ladies' lounge, adjusting the back seams on her sheer black stockings.

"How did women deal with these seams?" she asked, exasperated.

Gemma laughed. "They were just happy to have panty hose back then, I think."

Lillian narrowed her eyes with good humor. "You seem to have recovered well. What's with the good mood?"

"I didn't realize I was so morose," Gemma said dryly.

"Not morose, just….injured."

"I guess that's true," she murmured.

Lillian angled her head. "But you're better?"

Gemma did a gut check and was happy to find her heart at peace with the past. "Yes."

"And that lovely dark-haired man friend of yours, does he figure into it?"

"How did you know about him?"

Lillian waved her off. "That's not important. Do you love this guy?"

Gemma blinked. "Our relationship is just…physical."

"The importance of which is never to be underestimated," the older woman said. "But does your soul smile when he walks into the room?"

"I…I don't know. He makes me happy."

"Good. I'm glad I could see you happy before I leave."

Gemma frowned. "You're leaving?"

"They announced the exhibit will end in a couple of weeks, so I'm moving on to another temp job."

"The woman at my employment agency told me this could lead to another job in the museum."

"Maybe for someone with your background, but not mine. No, I'm off to my next adventure. But it has been a pleasure getting to know you." Lillian winked. "It's always nice to meet someone who shares particular interests. Good luck, Gemma. Always be true to yourself."

The woman's words stayed with her throughout the day. It was difficult to pinpoint the change in her, but as the tours progressed, she felt her mind expand to accept new possibilities for her future…and none of the options included compromise. She only hoped that it didn't mean she'd be lonely for the rest of her life.

When she arrived home, she marveled at the changes in the Spanish home just since the morning—the yard was newly sodded, with tree plantings and landscaping. The stucco walls of the house had been painted with an aged ochre that was a striking contrast to the red-tiled roof. Even though it was still daylight, the structure was illuminated inside and out. A caterer's truck sat next to the curb, along with a van from Party Balloons. Gemma smiled at the indulgences that reflected Chev's affection for his family and acknowledged a pang of regret for turning down his invitation to join them. But considering her last conversation with him, things would be way too awkward between them, and she didn't want to intrude on his family time.

Setting aside her disappointment, she hit the remote control and opened the garage door. The peacock wasn't around, but he had uprooted several clumps of daylilies. She sighed, then cut her wheel to pull into the right side of the garage. A split-second later, she frowned. Why was she still leaving room for Jason's car? Feeling magnanimous toward herself, she pulled into the center of the garage, leaving lots of breathing room on either side.

As the garage door was going down, she spotted the mailbox that still read Jason and Gemma White. "You're next," she announced.

She went inside, changed into casual clothes and grabbed the old suitcase containing her paints, then stopped in the garage for her hat and a garden trowel to replant the uprooted lilies. Outside, she inhaled the rich scent of an early summer evening. The sharp sweetness of new soil and grass rode the air from Chev's yard, tickling her senses.

Not Chev's yard, she reminded herself. The yard of whoever would buy the house in a couple of weeks. Most likely, a couple with children to enjoy the pool and the large family kitchen. Chev would pocket the money and move on to his next project—Miami, hadn't he said? And on to his next woman?

Of course he'd have another woman, and another after that. He was, after all, a hot-blooded, great-looking man with a healthy sexual appetite.

Who accepted her exhibitionism.

Who didn't judge her.

She exhaled, then plopped the hat on her head and walked to the mailbox at the curb. The honeysuckle bush she'd planted around the post was covered with fat buds that would soon burst with little cream-colored flowers and the most beautiful fragrance imaginable.

She remembered the day she'd painted their names on the mailbox. They had been in the house for less than a week. Jason seemed uninterested in anything having to do with the house and yard. She, on the other hand, had been eager to put their stamp on it, to make it theirs. He was working long hours, and she was in a nesting phase. She had bought a small can of black paint for metal surfaces and painstakingly painted on their names. Jason hadn't noticed and when she'd brought it to his attention, he had told her she could hire someone to do that kind of thing.

She took a deep breath and with a few strokes of a spray can, she obliterated their names with white primer, reducing the mailbox back to a clean, blank surface. She stared at it for a couple of minutes, then nodded. It felt right.

While she waited for it the primer to dry, she replanted the lilies, muttering under her breath about the peacock who seemed to be enamored with her yard. It had left behind two exquisite feathers. She set them on the porch to add to the others she had collected—they were simply too fine to throw away. A keepsake for the time after the bird had flown away.

Then she went back to the mailbox and, using a small brush and black paint, hand-lettered "Gemma Jacobs" on the side. She didn't realize she was holding her breath until the sight of it made her exhale in satisfaction.

She was putting the finishing touches on the paint job when two cars pulled into Chev's driveway. Doors opened and out came several people who obviously knew one another. When Chev came out to greet them, dressed in slacks and a collared shirt, there were shouts of joy and hugs all around. He shepherded them all into the house, then glanced in her direction.

Gemma couldn't look away. Even at this distance, she could feel the intensity of his regard.

He lifted his hand in a casual wave.

She waved back.

He hesitated a few seconds, then disappeared into the house.

And there it was…that achy emptiness in her stomach. And she realized in a blinding split second that she was letting something that could be incredible slip through her fingers. Sue was right—she was older now, and wiser. Old enough to recognize a good thing when it crossed her path. Wise enough not to pass up a chance to see a different side of this man she was falling in love with.

Having made up her mind, she couldn't shower and dress fast enough. For a hospitality gift, she settled on a vase of yellow and gold flowers cut from her garden. At the last minute, she added a peacock feather to the arrangement.

As she crossed her yard to Chev's, she was racked with nerves over seeing him again and meeting his family.

Funny how she was more comfortable performing as a stranger than as herself.

"ARE YOU OKAY, son?"

Chev looked up to see his mother walking toward him where he stood by the kitchen window overlooking the newly unveiled pool. Seeing his family again had lifted his spirits considerably, but it also had sharpened his awareness of missing Gemma. It shouldn't matter so much when he was leaving soon. But seeing her changing the name on her mailbox had left him feeling torn. If she wasn't going back to her ex…

The concern on his mother's sweet face made him smile. "I'm fine, Mama."

"You look sad."

"I'm just tired."

"It was nice of you to have this party for Maria, and to invite Juan and his family."

"I thought it would make you happy."

"It has. The house is beautiful. It will make someone a lovely home."

"I'm glad you like it, Mama."

"It reminds me of the house I grew up in."

"There's still plenty to do before the auction, but I think it's turned out well."

"So when will I see you settling down in a home of your own?"

He put his arm around his mother's shoulder and gave

her a squeeze. "Someday. Why don't we cut the cake? I know that Maria and Jeffrey are dying to get into the pool."

The sound of the doorbell cut through the air.

"Are you expecting someone else?" his mother asked slyly.

"Maybe," he said, perplexed. He excused himself and, as he walked toward the entrance, he allowed himself to hope that Gemma had changed her mind.

When he opened the door, her back was to him and she was scolding the peacock, which had apparently followed her over. Her efforts to shoo him away seemed only to provoke the blue bird because it unleashed a torrent of calls and unfurled his tail with a full-body shudder.

She turned back to the door, startled to see him standing there. "Hi."

"Hi," he said over the noise of the peacock, unable to mask an amused smile.

"Is there still room for one more? I promise to leave my friend outside."

"Absolutely," he said with a happy grin.

"We heard the noise," his mother said. "Oh, look!"

Everyone in his family came outside, exclaiming over the peacock, which seemed to know he had an audience and strutted like royalty around the colorful tiled walkway. Chev managed to introduce Gemma as the artist of the kitchen mural, and almost felt sorry for her under the onslaught of his boisterous parents, sister, aunt, uncle and cousin. His mother complimented the vase of flowers, then linked arms with Gemma and walked back inside.

His heart expanded in his chest, but he reminded himself that he couldn't get used to the idea of loving her. She had issues and at least one powerful reason to go back to her ex-husband, if she was afraid of what that reporter might reveal. And there was the little matter that in two weeks, he would be selling this house and leaving for Miami...

Determined to enjoy the day, he rejoined the party in the kitchen where the cake for his sister Maria who had graduated high school was being cut among choruses of cheers and singing. Chev glanced down the table where Gemma sat wedged between his mother and his aunt, and winked at her. She looked a little unsure of herself, but after a few minutes, she was laughing with everyone else.

After the cake had been devoured, his sister and cousin raced to change into their bathing suits. Chev watched for Gemma's reaction to the pool mosaic. She turned from the window with a look of wonder. "A peacock?"

He joined her there in the warmth of the sun and looked down at the sparkling blue water of the pool, dazzling against the design of a riotous peacock in the tile work of the bottom and sides. "It seemed fitting."

"It's beautiful. I wish I had brought my suit." Her green eyes danced mischievously.

Desire flooded his midsection. He leaned near her ear and whispered, "Why don't we have a private swim when everyone's gone?" He waited for her answer, needing to know if she had come to the party out of kindness, or for some other reason. "Unless you have other plans tonight," he added.

"No," she murmured. "I'm...free."

"What about your ex?"

"Still my ex."

"And the pictures the reporter took?"

She shrugged. "The guy's a jerk, but what can I do? I don't think it's anyone's business what I do for a living, but I've decided that I won't be ashamed if it gets out."

She was changed, he realized. She seemed stronger… braver. And if possible, sexier. Had the exhibitionism empowered her to make the decision not to go back to her ex? Or had something else figured into her decision?

Chev loved his family and enjoyed seeing Gemma interact with them, but as the hours passed, he grew more eager to be alone with her. When his family took their leave, he waved until the taillights of their cars disappeared, then turned and pulled her into his arms for a deep, thorough kiss. He wanted to have her now, against the wall, or in the grass. With a groan, he tore his mouth from hers. "Hold that thought. I need to run an errand."

A little frown marred her forehead. "Now?"

"Trust me—it can't wait."

"What about our swim?"

"Get your suit and wait for me at your house. I won't be gone long."

She sighed, then angled her head. "Okay. I'll be watching."

20

GEMMA DRESSED in a half-dozen different outfits waiting for Chev to return. Nothing seemed right…nothing seemed special. After an hour of indecision, she was struck with a panicky feeling that sex with Chev wouldn't be the same if she couldn't strip for him, or wear some sort of disguise.

If she couldn't pretend to be someone else.

Chev had accused her of using the exhibitionism as a way of avoiding emotional intimacy, and she couldn't deny it. He also said the two didn't have to be mutually exclusive. But she didn't see any way the two conditions could be reconciled.

Instead, she would simply enjoy the time she had left with Chev. He didn't have to know that she was falling for him.

So she settled on a skimpy black bikini with a short cover-up and high-heeled mules. And the mask…always the mask. She poured herself a glass of wine and drank deeply, feeding the languorous vibration that was already humming in her sex at the thought of performing for Chev. She had to admit that no stranger had ever fueled her lust to such heights. Knowing what lay in store for her in his arms made her feel loose limbed and expansive.

But how long would that feeling last? How long until

she yearned to perform for strangers again? She paced, alternately wanting answers and wanting options. Neither seemed clear or obvious…or satisfying.

It was getting late when Gemma heard his truck return. Mellow on wine, she lowered the mask in place and met him at the front door. With the light from the street behind him, she couldn't see his expression. But his low whistle got his point across. He reached for her hand and she allowed him to lead her outside to the glorious lit pool in his backyard. The going was precarious in the dark, especially with her wearing a mask and heels, but they laughed and stumbled their way through the grass.

The neighborhood was quiet and dark, with cicadas chanting in the background. Their sole attendant by the pool was the peacock, which seemed to enjoy watching the dappled surface. His head bobbed in time with the gentle slap of the water and he occasionally called out to a yet undiscovered mate.

Chev lowered himself to the edge of the pool next to a feather the bird had shed, removed his shoes and socks, and leaned back…to watch. Gemma obliged, shedding the cover-up first and walking around him suggestively. He reached for her, but she ducked away, then unhooked her bikini top and tossed it toward him. She crossed her arms over her breasts and turned back to face him, thrilled to see the bulge in his dark slacks. He pulled his shirt over his head and consumed her with his eyes.

The headiness of the wine and the sight of Chev's brown, bare torso sent ripples of excitement through her. She lifted her arms overhead, allowing her breasts to swing free, heavy and hard with need. She leaned over and shimmied off the bikini bottoms and threw those to him, too. He caught them neatly and brought them to his face, his eyes hooded. Then he picked up the peacock feather and pushed to his feet to stand before her.

Gemma stood perfectly still except for the rise and fall of her breasts. This man affected her body like a drug—she could hardly breathe, and her limbs seemed limp. His body was an inch from hers, his slacks and underwear the only clothes between them. Even barefoot he towered over her in heels. The dark springy hair on his chest tickled her erect nipples, his warm breath fanned her face. He lifted the feather and brushed it across her collarbone, over her breasts, down her stomach…and lower.

The velvety fringe was an erotic whisper over her sensitive folds, sending the most delicious sensations to her core. Behind the mask, she opened her mouth and sighed, looping her arms around his neck for support. He captured her mouth in a probing kiss and stroked her with the feather until she felt the moisture of her own lubrication on her thighs.

"Chev," she pleaded, fumbling with the fastener on his waistband. "Take me…now."

He helped her with his pants, stopping long enough to retrieve a condom from the pocket to sheath his rigid erection. Then he lifted her, wrapping her legs around his waist, and impaled her on his cock. Gemma gasped at the sensation of being filled with him, clawing at his back. He buried his head in her neck, grunting with every fierce stroke that joined their bodies more intimately, more savagely.

Her climax staggered her, crashed over her with a force that triggered every muscle in her body to contract involuntarily. She cried out his name and clung to him, disoriented because she felt as if she were falling.

"I've got you," he murmured, then grunted his own release, pumping into her while holding her against his chest. His strength alone was an aphrodisiac to her.

Afterward, he lowered her to the sweet, damp grass fringing the pool and eased his body from hers. "That was incredible," he murmured.

She moaned her agreement, thinking she'd love to lie here with him forever. He made her feel so alive, so feminine. She lifted his hand to her mouth for a kiss, then frowned at the torn skin on his knuckles. "Did you hurt your hand?"

He flexed it. "No. Just scraped it when I was loading some supplies earlier."

Her eyes had adjusted to the semidarkness, allowing her to study his body. "Does your tattoo have significance?" she asked, tracing her finger over the expansive branches and root system of the leafless tree.

He shrugged and craned to look at it. "What do you see?"

"Strength. And solitude."

"I guess that works," he agreed.

"Do you like your solitude?"

"Most of the time. But this is pretty nice."

She smiled in agreement.

"Although," he whispered, fingering the mask she still wore, "I wouldn't mind finding out more about the woman behind the mask."

Gemma swallowed hard.

She'd never met a man she felt so deeply connected to. But she also knew she couldn't—didn't want to—live without exhibitionism. Between her fetish and the fact that he was leaving soon, it was better to leave some things unsaid and unexplored.

CHEV FELT Gemma stiffen in his arms at the mention of losing the mask. She obviously wasn't comfortable enough with him to drop the pretense of the costume. Maybe she would never allow herself to be close to one man again.

Maybe it was best for him that he was leaving soon.

"How about that swim?" he suggested.

21

GEMMA LOVED to make love in the morning. She rolled over, and when she saw Chev lying next to her, she waited for lust to seize her.

Instead, love washed over her like a cleansing wave. She adored this man. He gave her joy…and hope. She reached out to touch the tattoo that spanned his deltoid muscle, reveling in the sensation of warm, smooth skin under her fingertips.

His eyes opened and he smiled at her, then clasped her hand, intertwining their fingers. She fought the sensation of shyness that descended in the daylight, without her mask and naked before him. Not an exotic, mysterious performer. Just Gemma.

"Last night was amazing," he murmured.

She could only nod, now nearly panicked by her burgeoning feelings for him. The phone rang and she moved to answer it, but he pulled her back.

"Stay with me," he urged.

She wanted to, but morning intimacy was so raw, so… *honest*. She was terrified it would break the spell. And then in a split second, she realized that breaking the spell might solve all her problems.

The machine kicked on. When she heard Jason's voice, she froze.

"Gemma, hey, it's me. Listen, I'm sorry if I was unkind on the phone the other day. I just had my hopes up, that's all. But you're right—we shouldn't get back together." He sighed heavily. "I also talked to Sue. She said she told you everything, and I'm sorry about that, too. More sorry than you'll ever know. I wanted to let you know that I called Wilcox to work out a deal on the photos. Funny thing is, he must have had a change of heart. He assured me that he'd destroyed the photos, said he didn't want to cause any trouble for you. Anyway, stay in touch. And Gemma...be happy."

Gemma smiled, abject relief flowering in her chest. "That's odd."

Chev rolled over and captured one soft nipple in his mouth. "What?" he murmured against her awakened skin.

"That Wilcox would have a change of heart about the photos. Why?"

"Who knows?" Chev murmured, traveling up to nuzzle her neck and covering her body with his. His thick erection pressed against her thigh.

A rogue thought popped into her mind. She frowned and lifted his right hand, the one with the scrapes across the knuckles. "Chev, did you go see Lewis Wilcox?"

"Maybe," he said, then kissed her ear.

Gemma gasped. "You beat him up?"

He ran his tongue along the sensitive cord of her neck. "I didn't have to. One punch and the guy was willing to negotiate."

"Negotiate what?"

Chev sighed and scratched his temple. "His cell phone and the promise that he wouldn't go public with the photos in return for his pretty TV face."

Shocked and flattered that Chev would stand up for her, she cupped his face in her hands. "You did that for me?"

"Yeah. I told him if he had a beef with your ex, he should take it up with him and keep you out of it."

Gemma smiled and whispered in his ear, "And what can I do for you?"

He nudged her sex with his. "You're doing it. No mask, no costumes. It's you that I want."

He entered her body to the tune of their mingled groans and made love to her slowly, his eyes locked with hers throughout. Watching his expression change with every nuance of heightened sensation opened her mind and body, magnified every touch, left her feeling out of control and hopelessly lost in him. This recklessness was like being disconnected from her physical self. She was powerless to do anything except go where his body took hers.

When her orgasm began to claim her, he urged her to the highest pinnacle she'd ever reached physically and emotionally. She came in a shattering clash, and carried him over the edge with her as he shuddered his release with full-body spasms. He cried her name over and over, pulsing inside her. Then he collapsed and rolled over, pulling her to his chest.

"I'm glad you're a morning person," he said, between re-covering breaths. "It's the best time of the day to have sex."

Gemma closed her eyes. She knew a sign when she saw one. "I love you," she blurted.

In the ensuing silence, she died a hundred deaths, wish-ing back her words. His hand traveled down her spine, over the curve of her hip. "I love you, too."

She lifted her head and stared at him, at his amazing eyes that spoke to her.

He sighed. "I feel a *but* coming on."

"The auction is in two weeks. You're leaving. And I have to be honest with you, Chev. Even though the job at the museum is ending soon, I don't know if I can ever let go of the watch-me games. It's…part of me."

He twined a strand of her hair around his finger. "So we have two weeks to see where this goes."

She nodded. An experimental period for them both to assess their options. This intense blaze they felt for each other might burn out. Or one of them could change their mind. They were both quiet, both lost in their own thoughts.

The two weeks stretched before Gemma like a big question mark.

"ARE YOU SURE you want me to do this?"

Gemma bit into her lower lip and nodded at Chev. "It's for the best."

His expression was pensive as he held the Auction Today sign with one hand and drove it into the ground with several whacks of the mallet. She stood back and looked at the sign, content with their decision.

A sedan pulled up next to the curb in front of the Spanish house. A suited man stepped out, along with a couple. "We're here for the auction?" he shouted.

"Change of plans," Chev said, waving them over. "This house is on the market instead—131 Petal Lagoon." He settled his arm around Gemma's shoulder. "Last chance to change your mind about moving in with me."

"Nice try," she said with a laugh. "As soon as my house sells, you're stuck with me."

Another car pulled up behind the first, then another. And it was still an hour before the auction. "What beautiful birds!" a woman exclaimed, obviously enchanted by the two peacocks strutting across Gemma's lawn. A peahen had arrived out of the blue, much to the cock's delight. They had become a celebrated pair in the neighborhood.

"Guess both of us cocks got lucky," Chev murmured to

her as he carried the mallet back to his pickup parked near her mailbox.

She elbowed him, but laughed. Then she spied a brown sack in the back of his truck and frowned. "What's that?"

Chev seemed flustered and tried to move the sack out of sight. "Nothing. Grass seed, I think."

She put her hands on her hips. "Let me see it."

He hesitated, then lifted the bag that read "Wild bird seed—for turkeys, pheasants and peacocks." The bag was almost empty.

Her eyes widened. "You were feeding it? *In* my yard?"

Chev gave her a sheepish smile and nodded.

"That's why I couldn't get rid of it!"

He shrugged. "A man's gotta do what a man's gotta do."

She punched him playfully, but he countered with a kiss. "Now that you're going to be a bigwig executive assistant to the director of the museum instead of a tour guide, if you get the urge to…you know, it's okay…as long as you come home to me."

"Always," she murmured, brimming with love for this sexy, sexy man.

"What's the letter?" he asked, pointing to the envelope she'd brought out with her.

She turned it over and smiled at the address. *Dr. Michelle Alexander.* "A thank-you to an old friend."

Gemma walked to the mailbox, wondering about the other young women in her Sex for Beginners class, where they were and if, like her, they'd received their fantasy letters at a pivotal point in their lives. And if, like her, they would use their letters to reclaim a part of themselves.

She hoped so. Because of her letter, the future lay before her, no longer a question mark, but a bold exclamation point.

Gemma placed the thank-you note in the mailbox, raised the flag and turned back to Chev, her heart full of him. She'd finally learned who she was. And she'd found a man who knew it—and loved it—too.

* * * * *

*Don't miss IN A BIND, the next blazing hot book
in the SEX FOR BEGINNERS trilogy
by Stephanie Bond, available next month.*

Here's a sneak peek at
THE CEO'S CHRISTMAS PROPOSITION,
the first in **USA TODAY** *bestselling author*
Merline Lovelace's **HOLIDAYS ABROAD** *trilogy*
coming in November 2008.

American Devon McShay is about to get the Christmas
surprise of a lifetime when she meets her new client,
sexy billionaire Caleb Logan, for the very first time.

Silhouette Desire

Available November 2008

Her breath whistled out in a sigh of relief when he exited Customs. Devon recognized him right away from the newspaper and magazine articles her friend and partner Sabrina had looked up during her frantic prep work.

Caleb John Logan, Jr. Thirty-one. Six-two. With jet-black hair, laser-blue eyes and a linebacker's shoulders under his charcoal-gray cashmere overcoat. His jaw-dropping good looks didn't score him any points with Devon. She'd learned the hard way not to trust handsome heartbreakers like Cal Logan.

But he was a client. An important one. And she was willing to give someone who'd served a hitch in the marines before earning a B.S. from the University of Oregon, an MBA from Stanford and his first million at the ripe old age of twenty-six the benefit of the doubt.

Right up until he spotted the hot-pink pashmina, that is.

Devon knew the flash of color was more visible than the sign she held up with his name on it. So she wasn't surprised when Logan picked her out of the crowd and cut in her direction. She'd just plastered on her best businesswoman smile when he whipped an arm around her waist. The next moment she was sprawled against his cashmere-covered chest.

"Hello, brown eyes."

Swooping down, he covered her mouth with his.

Sheer astonishment kept Devon rooted to the spot for a few seconds while her mind whirled chaotically. Her first thought was that her client had downed a few too many drinks during the long flight. Her second, that he'd mistaken the kind of escort and consulting services her company provided. Her third shoved everything else out of her head.

The man could kiss!

His mouth moved over hers with a skill that ignited sparks at a half dozen flash points throughout her body. Devon hadn't experienced that kind of spontaneous combustion in a while. A *long* while.

The sparks were still popping when she pushed off his chest, only now they fueled a flush of anger.

"Do you always greet women you don't know with a lip-lock, Mr. Logan?"

A smile crinkled the skin at the corners of his eyes. "As a matter of fact, I don't. That was from Don."

"Huh?"

"He said he owed you one from New Year's Eve two years ago and made me promise to deliver it."

She stared up at him in total incomprehension. Logan hooked a brow and attempted to prompt a nonexistent memory.

"He abandoned you at the Waldorf. Five minutes before midnight. To deliver twins."

"I don't have a clue who or what you're..."

Understanding burst like a water balloon.

"Wait a sec. Are you talking about Sabrina's old boyfriend? Your buddy, who's now an ob-gyn doc?"

It was Logan's turn to look startled. He recovered faster than Devon had, though. His smile widened into a rueful grin.

"I take it you're not Sabrina Russo."

"No, Mr. Logan, I am *not*."

* * * * *

Be sure to look for
THE CEO'S CHRISTMAS PROPOSITION
by Merline Lovelace.
Available in November 2008
wherever books are sold,
including most bookstores, supermarkets,
drugstores and discount stores.

MARRIED BY CHRISTMAS

Playboy billionaire Elijah Vanaldi has discovered
he is guardian to his small orphaned nephew.
But his reputation makes some people question
his ability to be a father. He knows he must
fight to protect the child, and he'll do anything
it takes. Ainslie Farrell is jobless, homeless and
desperate—and when Elijah offers her a position
in his household she simply can't refuse....

Available in November

HIRED: THE ITALIAN'S CONVENIENT MISTRESS

by

CAROL MARINELLI

Book #29

nocturne™

ESCAPE THE CHILL OF WINTER WITH TWO SPECIAL STORIES FROM BESTSELLING AUTHORS

MICHELE HAUF

AND

VIVI ANNA

WINTER KISSED

In "A Kiss of Frost," photographer Kate Wilson experiences the icy kisses of Jal Frosti, but soon learns that this icy god has a deadly ulterior motive. Can Kate's love melt his heart?

In "Ice Bound," Dr. Darien Calder travels to the north island of Japan, where he discovers an icy goddess who is rumored to freeze doomed travelers. Darien is determined to melt her beautiful but frosty exterior and break her of the curse she carries...before it's too late.

Available November wherever books are sold.

REQUEST YOUR FREE BOOKS!

2 FREE NOVELS
PLUS 2
FREE GIFTS!

⬥ HARLEQUIN®

Blaze™

Red-hot reads!

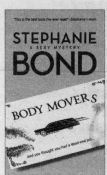
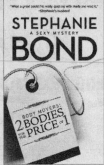

COMING NEXT MONTH

#429 KISS & TELL Alison Kent
In the world of celebrity tabloids, Caleb MacGregor is the best. Once he smells a scandal, he makes sure the world knows. And that's exactly what Miranda Kelly is afraid of. Hiding behind her stage name, Miranda hopes she'll avoid his notice. And she does—until she invites Caleb into her bed.

#430 UNLEASHED Lori Borrill
It's a wild ride in more ways than one when Jessica Beane is corralled into a road trip by homicide detective Rick Marshall. Crucial evidence is missing and Jess is the key to unlocking not just the case, but their pent-up passion, as well!

#431 A BODY TO DIE FOR Kimberly Raye
Love at First Bite, Bk. 3
Vampire Viviana Darland is in Skull Creek, Texas, looking for one thing—an orgasm. Or more specifically, the only man who's ever given her one, vampire Garret Sawyer. She knows her end is near, and wants one good climax before she goes. And she intends to get it—before Garret delivers on his promise to kill her....

#432 HER SEXIEST SURPRISE Dawn Atkins
He's the best birthday gift ever! When Chloe Baxter makes a sexy wish on her birthday candles, she never expects Riley Connelly—her secret crush—to appear. Nor does she expect him to give her the hottest night of her life. It's so hot, why share just one night?

#433 RECKLESS Tori Carrington
Indecent Proposals, Bk. 1
Heidi Joblowski isn't a woman to leave her life to chance. Her plan? To marry her perfect boyfriend, Jesse, and have several perfect children. Unfortunately, the only perfect thing in her life lately is the sex she's been having with Jesse's best friend Kyle....

#434 IN A BIND Stephanie Bond
Sex for Beginners, Bk. 2
Flight attendant Zoe Smythe is working her last shift, planning her wedding... and doing her best to ignore the sexual chemistry between her and a seriously sexy Australian passenger. But when she reads a letter she'd written in college, reminding her of her most private, erotic fantasies...all bets are off!

www.eHarlequin.com

HBCNM1008BPA